# CUSTER MEADOW

# CUSTER MEADOW

## Lauran Paine

**Walker and Company**
New York

First published in the United States of America
in 1988 by the Walker Publishing Company, Inc.

Published simultaneously in Canada by Thomas Allen & Son
Canada, Limited, Markham, Ontario.

Library of Congress Cataloging-in-Publication Data

Paine, Lauran.
  Custer Meadow.

  ISBN 0-8027-4072-3

  "A Walker western"
  I. Title.
PS3566.A34C87   1988     813'.54     87-21665

Printed in the United States of America

10 9 8 7 6 5 4 3 2 1

# CONTENTS

# CUSTER MEADOW

# CHAPTER 1
# One Man's Paradise

AT the higher elevations the golden and russet splash of autumn, with patches of red and orange and conifer green, cloaked forested areas to the east and west with a tumult of color, but lower down where black frost had not reached, the colors were a uniform shade of summer green above and tan below.

But even down there, while the days remained golden and warm, and occasionally downright hot, the grass was curing, its tawny color forming a carpet throughout the foothills that promised an end to summer.

But the sap was still running and fragrant, the dying blooms of wild flowers made a barely discernible vague perfume, and to the man astride the stud-necked bay ridgling it was the utter stillness with its lingering, slightly musty fragrance that signified the end of a season.

He came out of the forest onto the vast flow of Custer Meadow from the north, riding comfortably to the gait of his animal while absorbing the sights and scents of new country.

He thought he was in southern Colorado; at least the country looked the same as it had looked two hundred miles back through the mountains. But he knew that the boundary line between Colorado and northern New Mexico Territory ran through those mountains somewhere.

He was west of Raton Pass. In a crossroads village fifty miles back an old man had vaguely waved him southward in the direction of the trail he had found without difficulty and had followed through the mountains to this wide and long, high plateau. The old man had said he would come out of the timber atop a broad upland prairie known as Custer

1

Meadow, which was, according to the informant, the traditional route from north to south. The old man had studied the stranger with ancient eyes and had mildly said that if a man preferred not to travel ordinary routes, the trail to Custer Meadow would be best.

The old man had been right. For seven days the sturdy rider with a hint of gray at the temples had not seen a soul nor a habitation. Not even a pot hunter's cabin nor a stone ring where campfires had been made.

He had seen bear, cougars, wapiti higher up, and deer lower down, but no sign of people past or present.

He had taken his time and once, at a turquoise lake with lily pads larger than a hat, he had loafed away two golden days.

He was in no hurry, and although he was not accustomed to being lazy, those mountains at his back and the immense prairie-plateau in front made an idyllic resting place—the rider was in no haste to leave.

Wilderness fed the soul and eased the heartbeat. He had been four years building up a one-man cattle outfit in Wyoming with no days off. He had made it prosper against odds most men would have turned their backs on. But what made all the difference—he had sold it for more money than he had ever had before. It was under his shirt in a money belt.

Wyoming was a beautiful land, well-watered in summer, with miles of rolling grassland and timber, virgin country in all directions, but four Wyoming winters was enough. He had settled up, saddled up, turned his back on Wyoming and did not slow down until he was two-thirds down across Colorado heading for a country he had been told never had more than six inches of snow in wintertime, and summer nine months out of the year—the border territory between southern Colorado and northern New Mexico Territory.

For almost two days now he had known he was in it. He did not know exactly where he was, in the state or in the territory, and he did not care. He had emerged from seven days of magnificent mountainous country and now sat his patient ridgling on the edge of what he thought had to be Custer Meadow.

He dismounted, loosened the cinch, hobbled his horse and hung the bridle from the saddlehorn. While the ridgling dropped its head and grazed, the stocky rider with a heavy chestnut mane in need of shearing, knowledgeable, shrewd and good-natured blue eyes, squatted in lengthening shadows and rolled a smoke.

Everything he saw was pleasant. The autumn air was hot this far down from the high country. It had a hint of an edge to it, for though summer lingered months longer in this territory than it did back up in Wyoming, it was still subject to seasons.

After finishing his smoke, he strolled eastward in front of the mighty and mostly overripe, huge pines and firs, heard water and went looking for it. So far he had not once had to make a dry camp. The sound of a creek meant he would not have to tonight.

The creek came out of the timber on a dogleg bend around a bulging promontory of more big trees. As he went around the bulge and saw the water, he also saw a neck of land. A place where for some reason no trees grew, leaving a fairly wide and deep strip of land.

The creek was lively and about six feet wide. As the rider walked up to the bank, trout exploded in all directions when his shadow fell over the water.

He knelt, drank, removed his hat, scrubbed, drank some more and arose to go back for the ridgling, because this was where he intended to camp. What he had not seen at first because of mottled shadows was a log shack set as close to the northwesterly fringe of timber as its builder could put it without clearing land.

The rider stood looking back. He had to go no closer to realize it was a very old log cabin. Its walls, however, were still square and plumb, though its roofline had the barest hint of sag, the leather door-hinges had rotted, and the handmade door was flat on the ground with grass growing around it. There were window holes but no glass. There had never been any glass. When that cabin had been built, windows were made of clear rawhide scraped almost paper-thin. People could not see in or out, but clear rawhide let sunlight in.

He went back for the ridgling, led it toward the cabin, removed the rigging, rehobbled the horse, and with saddle, blanket and bridle draped over a shoulder walked up onto the rotting porch under its narrow overhang roof.

He stopped dead still. It had never occurred to him that the old trapper's shack, or whatever it was, might be inhabited. He had not looked for sign and therefore had not seen any, but now there was a definite but very faint scent of cooking: fried meat and coffee.

He eased the saddle to the ground, pushed the carbine boot to one side and without entering the shack turned very slowly to look in all directions. He had seen no trampled grass on the way into the neck, and now he saw none anywhere else.

He eased around behind the cabin. There had been a pole corral back there. Now, two-thirds of it was rotting in the grass. But there was fresh horse sign. In fact, from the amount of it, he guessed whoever had been here must have stayed for several days.

He went back around front, hauled his outfit inside, upended the saddle in a corner, and turned to study the room. It was fairly large for a log cabin. There was a mortared stone fireplace and cooking area in one corner. On both sides were surprisingly well-made cupboards, and against the west wall was an old bunk which originally had rope springs, though mice and wood rats had pretty well taken care of the rope. On the earthen floor beside the bunk someone had unfurled a blanketroll. The imprints in the dust were very clear, as were boot tracks. In a corner near the doorway was an Indian broom. Not an old one, either, so whoever had camped here earlier had been a tidy individual who liked cleanliness. That, the rider told himself, probably set this feller apart from a thousand other range-riders.

There was a small sack of flour and half a tin of baking powder in one of the cupboards. There was also a nearly empty little bag of ground coffee. The rider found a patched bucket, took it down to the creek and returned with it. There was kindling so he made a fire, heated water, and shaved. But he did not touch the coffee or the flour and baking powder, although the idea of hot biscuits was a strong temptation. He had his own little bag of coffee.

He settled in, ate a meager meal, and went outside for a smoke and a walk out to where the horse was. Since childhood he had been a solitary individual, the kind who talked to animals.

The horse paid no attention. He was accustomed to being spoken to, and if he thought about it at all, he perhaps suspected that was how two-legged things breathed, by making noises with their mouths.

Like most ridglings, it was a one-man horse. It had more intelligence, more stamina, and more fighting ability than other horses; and because of that fighting instinct—which went with its stud-horse instincts—it could not be turned loose around geldings and mares, especially mares. But since ridglings looked like geldings to casual observers, and some who were not so casual but who were ignorant as hell, an awful lot of corralled livestock had been badly bitten and kicked by ridglings.

For a one-man horse, there was no better saddle animal. This ridgling's name was Ulysses S. Grant, U.S. for short. It knew its name and it liked the company of the muscular blue-eyed man who rode it, but this afternoon it was too hungry to be bothered. Riding through big timber might feed a man's soul but it put pleats in a horse's gut because grass would not grow in earth which was two-thirds rock and one-third resin.

The sun went first, then some of the daylong warmth departed. The rider led his horse back closer to the shack, rehobbled him, and stamped across the rotting wood of the porch and stepped inside.

There was only one sound: someone cocking a sixgun alongside the front wall, beside the door behind the rider. He stopped without even breathing for a couple of seconds.

A tenor voice roughened by the situation, said, "Drop the gun!"

The rider dropped it.

"Who are you; what are you doing here?"

The rider answered without so much as moving his head. "My name is Ellis Bowman. I came onto this place after riding out of the northward mountains from Colorado."

"You've never been on Custer Meadow before?"

"Never have. Do you live here, mister?"

"For now I do." There was a long pause then the sound of a gunhammer being eased down before the lanky silhouette back by the doorless opening said, "Do you know where you are, Mister Bowman?"

"Custer Meadow. An old man in a town up north told me where the trail through the mountains was, and the name of a big meadow I'd find at the end of it. I was aiming for New Mexico, but if this plateau isn't down there, why then I expect I'm still in Colorado."

The silhouette remained in shadows. "Turn around."

They made their private and individual assessments of each other. The silhouette was about as tall as Ellis Bowman and seemed less thick and massive, but it was difficult to be sure of that because of the hip-length big old blanket-lined coat. The face had fine features, a straggly mustache much darker than the lighter hair showing beneath an old hatbrim, the eyes the shade of dark slate.

Bowman smiled. "I'll move my things outside, mister."

The gunman holstered his weapon and seemed to take a long time considering his reply. "No need. Have you eaten?"

"Yeah."

"Well, I haven't . . . I've been over near the south rim. There is a town down there. Did you know that?"

"No sir. Fact is I thought I'd found virgin country. It's a hell of a big meadow isn't it?"

"Yes. Once, there were cattle and horses up here. Now, they don't even free-graze it because down below around Batesville there's enough feed without pushing cattle up this far."

"You got a name, friend?"

The silhouette nodded and while keeping distance between them, went around toward the fireplace where pale red coals still glowed. "Sam Hanks. My paw was the cousin of President Lincoln's wife."

Ellis watched Sam Hanks work at the hearth and repeated his offer to bed down outside. Hanks looked around with a faint scowl. "No. You sleep inside on the floor, over by the back wall. . . . There are bears around. I've heard stories of 'em eating men in their bedrolls."

Ellis went thoughtfully to his saddle to untie his blankets and ground cloth. He had heard those tales too, and other ones he did not believe either, like hoop-snakes, critters that took their tails in their mouths and rolled like a buggy tire. If a bear ate a sleeping man, the man would have to be sleeping more soundly than Ellis Bowman had ever slept.

The feeling Ellis got was that for some reason Sam Hanks did not want him out of sight.

# CHAPTER 2
# Surprise!

AS night paled out toward dawn, it was a long time before sunrise came because of an overcast sky. Being an individual who had arisen with the sun or shortly before its arrival, Ellis Bowman went right on sleeping even after sunrise because of that continuing gloom. There was no sunlight when he opened one eye, as someone roughly shook him.

Then he opened the other eye. A big bearded man in a sheep-pelt riding coat was bending over with a sixgun in his gloved fist. When the big man saw Bowman's eyes open, he cocked the sixgun.

There were four other men inside the cabin, expressionless, grim-mouthed, eyes fixed on the man in the bedroll. Those four were clean-shaven. One of them was holding Bowman's saddlegun in a loose grip. The others had their coats open and brushed back to expose holstered Colts.

Ellis groaned and pushed slowly up into a sitting position.

The coiled shellbelt and holstered sixgun he had carelessly tossed within reach before retiring were not there. His boots and hat were, though. He eyed the four motionless men near the doorway, and turned again to regard the big bearded man and his cocked gun.

The large man straightened up and stepped back. "Get out of there an' stand up," he said in a deep voice that came out of a massive chest. "And be real careful."

Ellis looked at the big man without moving. Beneath the bedroll he was fully clothed but unarmed and bootless. As he rolled the blankets off and pushed upright some of the cobwebs dissipated. He faced the big man with a question. "Mind if I put my boots on?"

8

One of the other men stepped over, upended each boot, then tossed them down. "Put 'em on," he growled and moved back.

The bearded man eased down the hammer of his gun but did not holster it. "Who are you?" he asked.

"Ellis Bowman. I found this cabin yesterday afternoon." He looked around the room. There was no sign of Sam Hanks. Even his bedroll was gone.

The big man had another question. "Is that your sorrel horse hobbled out front?"

Ellis started to nod then checked the impulse. "He's not sorrel, he's bay."

The big man looked at his companions, then back. "He's sorrel, mister."

Ellis settled both feet into his boots and moved slightly until he could see out the doorless opening. There was a rawboned big sorrel horse out there, hobbled and cropping grass, ignoring five saddled horses tied up out front and the men who had ridden them.

Ellis let his breath out slowly and faced the bearded man again. "That's not my horse, mister. I rode in here on a bay ridgling branded EB on the left shoulder."

One of the onlookers snorted. "There ain't no horse with a shoulder brand out there."

Ellis stared at the speaker, who was burly and unshaven and had coarse, thick features. He looked around the room again. His little dented blueware coffeepot was on the hearth. Right now he could use some black coffee. He could have used a drink of whiskey but he had none. "Mind telling me who you gents are?" he said mildly.

The bearded man lowered his gun and pulled back one side of his coat. There was a steel circlet pinned to his shirtfront with a little silver star inside it. "I don't mind," he said dourly. "Those there are possemen. I'm Marshal Will Thompson from down at Batesville. And you are the gent we couldn't track last night in the dark, but caught up with this mornin' as soon as a man could made out tracks. Mister, that was a damn fool thing to do—stop to sleep. Anyone in your boots with a lick of sense wouldn't even have slowed down for a week." Marshal Thompson studied Ellis Bowman through an interval of cold silence, then said. "Where is it; did you hide it around here somewhere or you got it in them saddlebags?"

Before Ellis could reply a lanky man with an unfriendly face pointed. "There's somethin' under his shirt, Will."

Marshal Thompson looked, then said, "Peel out of the shirt. Starin' at me ain't going to do you any good. I said peel out of that shirt or I'll rip it off you. *Now!*"

Ellis's mind was working normally by now, but not very well as he reluctantly began removing the shirt. All the money he had in the world—except the coins in his pocket—was next to his belly in that leather belt with the little pockets. And there was a lot of it. To him anyway. They had his guns. They also had their own guns and—lawmen or not—getting possession of his money could turn them into something besides posse riders and a town marshal.

He hadn't mentioned Sam Hanks. He did not mention him now as the big man signaled for him to hand over the moneybelt, but he was beginning to have some very uncharitable thoughts about Sam Hanks, because for a clear fact Hanks was the person these men wanted.

Marshal Thompson stepped closer to daylight and begun opening the little moneybelt-pockets. His four companions crowded up to watch. If Ellis had had a gun at this one moment, he could have shot them all. But he did not even know where his sixgun was.

Marshal Thompson counted laboriously, then raised menacing eyes as he said, "It's all here an' a little bit more . . . Cowboy, put on your hat, walk out of here in front of us, and saddle your sorrel horse. We got ten miles to ride, and we'd like to make it before dinnertime. *Walk!*"

Ellis did not move. "Where do you think that money came from?" he asked the bearded man.

"From Turner's bank down at Batesville. The son of a bitch who robbed the bank was ridin' that sorrel horse out front and—"

"What did he look like, Marshal?"

Thompson finished buckling the belt and slung it carelessly over his shoulder as he answered. "He looked like you, mister."

Ellis shook his head. "No he didn't. He was thinner and had a mustache."

A posseman fished in his coat pocket then held out a gloved hand with a little tuft of dark brown hair on his palm. "While you was sleeping," he said, "we picked this off the floor."

Thompson was not a patient individual. "Walk out of here!"

The sun had not yet burned through that high overcast. Ellis approached the sorrel, swore to himself, and as he was kneeling to remove the hobbles he said, "Does the name Sam Hanks mean anything to you gents?"

No one replied but behind Bowman's back the possemen exchanged a look.

"When I rode in yesterday there was a man here who said his name was Sam Hanks. This isn't my horse. I didn't see the other horse but this has got to be it." Ellis stood up facing the possemen, and told them everything that had transpired yesterday afternoon and evening. When he was finished Marshal Thompson pointed. "Throw the saddle on him and shut up."

Ellis looked from face to face. There was not one that showed any interest in what he had just said. He saddled the sorrel horse getting angrier by the moment. When the six of them were mounted one of the possemen led off, riding westward into the timber. Behind Ellis Bowman rode the big town marshal, his eyes fixed on his prisoner's back. Bringing up the rear was another man, shorter by a head though about the same age as the marshal, maybe forty-five or fifty, and badly weathered, as though he had spent most of life in all kinds of sun and heat, cold and ice, wind and rain. He worked his jaws slowly on a cud of chewing tobacco.

Once he spat and said, "Will, I don't believe there ever was one with the sense gawd gave a goose. In his boots I'd have been fifty miles up through them mountains by now."

Will Thompson did not say a word, but as they were crossing a five-acre glade of grass and charred stumps he fished out a large watch, opened it, studied the time, snapped it closed and returned it to his pocket.

Ellis had a lot of time to think. Every way he found to consider his present situation came out bad. Sam Hanks was a damned bank robber. He'd said the reason he had got back late to the cabin was because he had been over on the west side of the plateau. The town Bowman was being taken to was in that direction, but down off the plateau in the lower grassland country.

A wizened scarecrow of a posseman, over six feet tall which made him seem even more scrawny, looked around and said, "You're lucky, cowboy. I've seen men hangin' in trees for less'n what you did."

Ellis eyed the narrow, lantern-jawed face. "I'll tell you the gospel truth, mister, and you wouldn't believe it if I was straddlin' ten feet of Bibles. I've never seen your town, didn't know there was a bank within five hundred miles of this meadow, and I sure as hell did not rob it. But if I had, do you think I'd be dumb enough to be sleeping in that shack back yonder this morning?"

The scarecrow smiled to expose teeth stained brown from years of tobacco chewing. "Yeah, I think you'd be that dumb. I've never in my life seen an outlaw who had any more sense than to do something that stupid."

At the edge of the plateau there was a steep trail, wide and evidently very old because in places where it passed through patches of granite, the trail was worn to a depth of about ten inches. It was fairly steep and it clung to the nearly perpendicular barranca all the way down from the meadow to some uneven, indifferently wooded low and round foothills which formed the base of the high plateau.

There was tall grass down there, and the sun finally burned through to bounce off the cliff-face, reflecting its heat against the men and horses.

The lead rider angled southeast, setting a course which had previously been marked by riders trampling down grass stalks as they passed.

When they came to a wide expanse of churned earth one of the possemen looked back at the town marshal. "You was right," he said. "If I'd have shot that rattlesnake last night the sound would have carried up yonder. If it had, we'd be ridin' back empty-handed."

Will Thompson's grim expression did not relax but he nodded with a satisfied expression showing briefly. He was a man of considerable self-esteem. It always made him feel better when folks recognized the fact that he was never wrong.

The first thing Ellis Bowman saw of Batesville was a tall windmill tower. The flukes were not turning; there was no breeze to turn them, and it grew increasingly hot as they came closer to the town.

Batesville had trees, obviously planted by hand since there were no trees anywhere else on the open range within sight of town. It was an attractive place, situated where four wagon roads converged near a large spring that gushed water year round. Half of it had been channeled into town, the other half coursed southward down a deep gully that made its crooked way under several old wooden bridges. One of the bridges was exceptionally wide, probably to accommodate drives of cattle.

Most of the buildings in Batesville were made of logs. Some had been sheathed in planed lumber, which made them look newer, and there were several structures of red brick. One was a place with thick steel shutters that could be locked in front of glass windows. It had a neatly painted legend in a half-moon shape above the roadside door: Batesville Stockmen's Bank.

The sun had burned off the veil-like overcast when the lead rider turned directly down the center of Main Street. He sat his saddle like he had a ramrod up his back, looking neither left nor right to where surprised pedestrians stopped to stare.

A fat man emerged from a poolhall and yelled to Marshal Thompson. "Done it again, eh, Will?"

Thompson turned his head and nodded.

By the time they halted at the tierack out front of the Batesville jailhouse, people were moving again, some in small groups where they held animated conversations. Ellis dismounted when someone growled for him to do so, and was herded into a large log building whose inside office smelled of old tobacco smoke, human sweat, and leather. The building was in the middle of town on the west side of the road. In wintertime when there was sunlight, it was warm no matter how cold it was outside. The log walls were about fifteen inches thick and there was only one small, barred window recessed in the front wall. The possemen were gruffly dismissed and went in a bunch to The Waterhole Saloon. Their experience and what they had to tell would ensure that they would not have to buy a single shot of whiskey.

A few idlers stood across the road in front of the Batesville Emporium—Leather Goods Bolt-Cloth and Victuals—facing the jailhouse making the usual groundless speculations, but by supper time the story would have been told and retold throughout town. Marshal Will Thompson had done it again.

# CHAPTER 3
## Batesville

ELLIS Bowman's cell smelled of carbolic acid. It was large enough for two prisoners and had bunks built against the north and south walls. There was a window about eighteen inches wide, twenty-four inches in length, higher in the roadside wall than a man could reach without a chair to stand on, and it had bars as thick as a man's thumb set into it. When the sun was on the east side of town, light and warmth came through that little window; otherwise, the cell was dingy and in wintertime as cold as a witch's bosom.

The only furniture consisted of a three-legged milking stool. Ellis used it to stand on so he could see as much of Batesville as the thick log walls on both sides permitted him. He was standing like that when someone opened the massive oaken door from the marshal's office and started down the corridor. Ellis climbed down and faced around as Will Thompson stooped to shove a tin plate with hash on it, and a tin cup of water under the door. As the lawman straightened he looked in impassively at his prisoner.

He had the saddlebags, the bedroll, and everything except the ridgling saddle horse that his prisoner owned, in his office. Including the seller's copy of the sale-deed to a ranch up in Wyoming, which was carefully folded between the sheets of a letter from a man named Ephraim Gottlieb who owned a general store in a place called Runnymede showing that the indebtedness of one Ellis Bowman at the Runnymede General Store had been paid in full.

These things and some personal effects such as an old straight razor, a change of underwear, and half a box of carbine bullets, had been in the prisoner's saddlebags, but, as the big lawman with the fixed expression of impersonal coldness gazed at his prisoner, he appeared to Ellis Bowman no different than when he had been back at Sam Hanks' damned cabin.

When Thompson spoke his tone was the same; unfriendly and gruff. "Are you a drinker, Mister Bowman?"

"Now and then. If it's real cold out, and maybe around Christmas time, a little."

Thompson continued to look balefully through the steel straps. "Are you sure you never been in this country before?"

"I'm sure, Marshal."

"Then how's it come you used that old In'ian trail to come out on Custer Meadow? Why didn't you use the regular road?"

Ellis told him about the old man up north who had explained where the trail was. Marshal Thompson was not satisfied. He said, "All right. And maybe whoever told you about that old trail knew you didn't want to ride down to Batesville out in plain sight. Folks might recollect seein' you."

Ellis crossed closer to the front of his cell. "You got my saddlebags?"

"Yes."

"Did you look through them? Marshal, I didn't rob your bank. I didn't know there was a town anywhere around here because it's new country to me. If you went through my saddlebags, you found a paper saying I sold my ranch up north. That's true. And because I didn't want to put in one more winter in Wyoming, I started south looking for a country where snow don't get hip-pocket high on a tall Indian every damned winter . . . That paper told you where I got that money I had in a belt under my shirt . . . Marshal, you're not going to find the feller who rode that rough-looking sorrel horse unless you get on his trail, while there still is a trail."

Will Thompson's features showed the faintest of sardonic expressions. "Sam Hanks?"

"Yes. Sam Hanks."

"Cowboy, I think you been in this country before, but maybe not long enough to do much more'n scout up our bank. Otherwise you'd know there ain't no Sam Hanks . . . Sam Hanks had a ranch in the foothills years ago. His wife's buried out there, alongside their baby son. Sam Hanks got himself kicked to death some years back. He's buried in the cemetery east of town. That old cabin was where he lived years back before he quit trappin' and went to raising beef . . . Maybe you believe in ghosts, cowboy, but I don't, and neither do those men who was with me yesterday when we caught you, an' you spun that yarn about Sam Hanks being at the cabin . . . By the way, old Hanks didn't have a mustache, he had a full beard and it was as white as snow, not dark brown . . . Cowboy, you're a real fancy liar. Now eat your meal. I'll be back when I get around to it."

Ellis ate what he thought was probably the scrapings of other meals served at the cafe. But the water was good. Afterwards he settled full length on one of the bunks and with both hands clasped under his head stared at the ceiling. He did not believe in ghosts either but, as an acquaintance had once observed, no one believes in ghosts until they see one. Just one; that'd be all it'd take to make a believer out of a man.

Except that Sam Hanks hadn't been a ghost, and he hadn't had a white beard. He had looked to be about twenty-five years old. That left one explanation. Whoever had robbed the Batesville bank had used Sam Hanks' name. It couldn't have been anything else—except that whoever he was, he was not a stranger to this area. If he had been, it was doubtful that he'd have known about the real Sam Hanks, and that led Ellis Bowman into a wider area of speculation. An almost limitless one, in fact.

He put those speculations aside long enough to consider his situation—and the town marshal. By now, sure as hell, he had gone through Ellis's saddlebags, had found that paper telling about the sale of his land up north.

But Thompson had not mentioned it. Twelve thousand dollars, which was what he'd had in his moneybelt, would be a hell of a temptation even to someone who didn't look as mean and conniving as Marshal Thompson.

For twelve thousand dollars a lot of men, with badges and without them, would commit murder. Ellis Bowman was a stone around the marshal's neck. Thompson could be relied upon to tell his story at every opportunity, which included when he was arraigned before a judge on a charge of bank robbery.

Mostly, he probably would not be believed, but people in towns and courtrooms had long memories. They might even be influenced by what he had to say, and his piece of paper from up north about the sale of his ranch should clinch it.

Ellis Bowman felt like a rat in a trap.

The longer he thought like this, the more it worried him. Would he live to face a judge in a roomful of spectators? Maybe he would. Maybe he had made an incorrect judgment about Will Thompson; but if he hadn't, he was likely to end up under a pile of stones deep in the mountains where his carcass might never be found.

He sat up on the edge of the bunk. The cell door was reinforced strap steel and was secured on the outside by a brass padlock as thick as a man's hand.

That slit of a window, even if it hadn't been barred from the outside, was too narrow for a man of Bowman's build to squeeze through.

He had plenty of time to make a careful study of his surroundings, and the ultimate conclusion he came to was that whatever this building had once been—perhaps part of an army stockade and brig—since its construction it had been modified a number of times, clearly with a view to make it absolutely escape-proof. Even a stick of dynamite would not blow a hole in those mighty log walls, and if he'd had one he'd have to be crazy to use it in a cell no larger than this one. The explosion would blow him out into the corridor.

His pockets had been emptied in Marshal Thompson's office. He had been allowed to keep only his handkerchief and tobacco sack.

The floor underfoot was grouted slabs of rock. It occurred to him that probably no one had ever escaped from the Batesville jailhouse, but if one had, he'd had a lot more experience with jailhouses than Ellis Bowman had. Ellis had never been a prisoner before in his life.

He considered the steel door, and doubted that a one-ton bull could have crashed through it. Still, the door was his only way out.

He thought of Marshal Thompson, who was big enough to wear a saddle, never came down the corridor without his gunbelt, and did not even open the door to feed his prisoner. Attacking Will Thompson would be about as likely to be successful as attacking a boar-bear.

Ellis arose and walked over to rattle the door with one hand, study its construction and the way large steel bolts had been heated and bent upright to hold it, then smashed flat on top so the door could not be lifted off its hangers.

He returned to the center of the cell and studied the narrow window briefly before turning back to face the door. Sooner or later, one way or another, that was how he was going out, either with Thompson's cocked sixgun in his back when he was herded to a court hearing, or some other way.

He returned to perch on the edge of the bunk and gaze murderously at the stone floor. Sam Hanks! By now he'd be fifty miles away with no one tracking him. In another few days he could be up in Colorado, or heading west toward Idaho. Or perhaps east toward Nebraska. Ellis had had his share of confrontations; it was impossible for a man to live as long as he had lived and not have them, but he had never killed a man in anger, had in fact only twice drawn his gun against another human being. Both those times had been against cattle thieves. But if he ever met Sam Hanks again, he would kill him.

Someone opened the big oak door up front. Ellis looked around as the heavy stride of Marshal Thompson echoed ahead. When he halted out front to look in, his face was as expressionless as it usually was. He spoke in a flat tone of voice. "Ain't all the money there. Mister Turner from the bank counted it with me. It's short three thousand dollars. You want to tell me where you cached it, or do I overhaul your carcass an' find out that way?"

Ellis sat as still as a stone. One thing was very clear. Up at the cabin Thompson had said all the money was in the moneybelt and his possemen had heard him say it. He had even said there was a little more money than had been taken from the Batesville bank.

Now he had just said it was not all there. He was lying.

When the prisoner simply sat on his bunk gazing out at him without saying a word, Marshal Thompson's face reddened. Without taking his pale eyes off the prisoner, Marshal Thompson pulled the riding gloves from under his shellbelt and put them on very slowly. His purpose in doing this was obvious even before he took the big brass key from a pocket and started to unlock the cell door.

Ellis was shorter than Thompson, and although there was considerable hard muscle punched down inside his hide, he was also at least twenty pounds lighter. Ellis had brawled and was no novice at it, but Marshal Thompson was one of those lawmen who had been beating prisoners to a pulp for years as part of his job. He would be very experienced at that sort of thing.

Ellis had learned from hand-fighting that there was one unarguable rule: Don't wait, don't hesitate. No one ever won a fistfight or any other kind of a fight by defending himself. As the brass key turned in the big lock, Ellis came up off the bunk and walked forward. Marshal Thompson stopped turning the key and looked at the powerfully built man five feet away. The prisoner had just spoiled one of Will Thompson's tried and proven methods of attacking. Ellis was about a foot too far back to be struck violently when Thompson threw all his weight into the door as it swung inward.

A loud voice from up front called out. "Will? You down in the cell-room?"

Thompson was still holding the key in the lock. He did not turn his head nor seem aware that someone was up in his office until the visitor called again. "Will! It's Charley Turner."

Thompson relocked the door, withdrew the key and without modifying his venomous look, turned up the corridor, removing his gloves as he went. He'd had no illusions; beating Bowman would not be easy, but Will Thompson had faced men before who had been just as challenging and he had succeeded every time.

He was entering the office when his expression began to relax. He nodded to the portly, graying man over by his desk, turned and locked the cell-room door, then went around behind his desk, which was actually a large table. As he sat down eyeing the banker he said, "I'll have a confession out of him directly. Just now he dug in his heels, but he'll confess. Maybe not for a day or two . . . Charley, what's on your mind?"

The portly, graying man went to a bench. "When we counted that money, and put aside what was over an' above what was robbed from the bank, I kept having a bad feeling. So a little while ago I talked to my clerk . . . Will, you got that money handy?"

Marshal Thompson turned in his chair and leaned down to work the dial on a small steel safe which had been painted light gray, and had a fat child painted on the door, naked and dimpled, except for a kind of floating scarf it was trailing in front which the artist had no doubt put in the picture to avoid giving offense.

When Thompson turned back with the moneybelt, he

wordlessly opened one of the little pockets and unfolded the greenbacks atop his desk. Then he raised questioning eyes to the portly man with the blue shirt and necktie. "You want to count it again?" he asked.

Charley Turner stared at the money and shook his head. He did not even arise to walk closer for half a minute, then, as he did this, he studied the greenbacks more closely and with an almost doleful wag of his head, said, "Will . . . That can't be the money that was stolen from the bank."

Marshal Thompson's eyes widened on the graying man. "What the hell are you talking about? It's the damned money. I took it off that feller I captured yesterday and fetched back to town."

The banker returned to his bench. "I know. I was sure it was too . . . When I got back to the bank my clerk was standing there, so I told him all about the moneybelt, that money lyin' there, and the prisoner you had in your cells."

"Well, what of it?"

". . . The money stole from the bank day before yesterday had been counted-in and signed for by my clerk. It came directly to us from the Denver mint. It was brand spankin' new money. Didn't have a crease in any of it. Look at this money. It's old, been crushed and worn and looks like it's passed through maybe four or five hundred hands and pockets . . . Until the clerk asked if it was fresh-made money I didn't know the money that was stolen was new as a fresh-born baby."

Marshal Thompson's face was as blank as the stare he held upon the man across from him.

The banker fished for a white handkerchief and dabbed his face and neck with it. As he was putting away the handkerchief he said, "That's not the stolen money, Will. I'd like to talk to your prisoner."

Thompson's astonishment had passed. Without speaking or looking up he began to methodically fold the notes and put them back into the belt. As he was turning to place the belt back into his safe he said, "Charley, it's got to be the same money. It's within about nine hundred dollars of the same amount." He slammed the door, spun the dial and faced around again. "He was riding the sorrel horse folks saw the stranger run out of town on." Thompson leaned with big hands clasped atop his desk.

Turner was very uncomfortable, and for a number of reasons, of which the possibility that Marshal Thompson had brought in the wrong man was only one. Charles Turner had known Will Thompson for about eight years. He had in fact been on the town council when it was decided to employ Thompson as a replacement for the former town marshal who had retired and left the country. He knew Will Thompson. After eight years, Charley Turner knew two particular things about Marshal Thompson: He could never be wrong, and he was a physically violent individual. He mopped his face and neck again, then arose from the bench.

He mentioned the other thing that was bothering him. "Will, if that's not the same money, why then you got to have the wrong man locked up . . . And the real outlaw is getting away."

For fifteen minutes after the banker had departed, Marshal Thompson sat totally motionless. Then he smiled.

# CHAPTER 4
# Saturday in Batesville

THE next day was Saturday. Thompson brought Bowman breakfast, then departed without a word. It was the noise that eventually attracted Ellis to the narrow high window. There were people and wagons, horsemen and dust. He watched for a while, then got down and decided it had to be Saturday. He rarely kept track of days. In fact, when he came out of the mountains onto Custer Meadow he had not been sure what month it was.

But anyone who had been part of one of those Saturday processions with a wagon and team and a long list of supplies would have recognized the same thing no matter where he was. The clear proof was the number of ranch women and scrubbed youngsters who were on the street.

Batesville rang with calls back and forth among stockmen and their riders who had not seen each other in a long while. Horses squealed along tieracks and there was a sound of someone at the blacksmith's shop warping a bar of steel across an anvil, probably replenishing a depleted stock of caulked horseshoes. Ranchers and riders could, and commonly did, shoe their own horses, but it was a dirty, rough, and unpleasant chore. If it could be put off until someone rode or drove his horse to town, for fifty cents the local smith would do it.

Once there was a furious dogfight accompanied by the hooting of yelling onlookers. Then someone, probably the big lawman, broke it up, and the arrival of a stagecoach from the east provided a diversion. It was the custom to stand, or lean in the shade and solemnly watch passengers alight, trying to guess something about them, and discuss their dress, or their general appearance. If there was a handsome woman or two among the newcomers, the rangemen made subdued rooster sounds, then laughed.

Saturday in a cowtown could be the longest day in the week for merchants, saloonmen, the local marshal, and for the local medical man, if there was one, which there was not in Batesville. But there was an old man named Cuthbert who had a dingy little apothecary shop south of the bank and north of the saddle and harness works. Old Cuthbert gave advice on illness, set broken bones, even looked after ring-bones, spavins and, most common, collar-galls on horses.

At the cafe, operated by a cadaverously thin man who rarely spoke and never smiled, business was brisk all the long day. At Wheeler's saloon, called The Waterhole, the proprietor was more congenial even though by dusk his feet would be killing him. He had half-frozen them one time with the result that impaired circulation bothered him if he stood for hours on end. He had once told Jed Cuthbert that for a long time he had thought making the kind of profit he made on Saturdays was worth the pain, but lately he was beginning to think that was wrong as hell. The apothecary had sold the barman a new concoction in a beautiful little square blue bottle whose purpose, as stated on the label, was the "dilation of arteries, enhancement of masculine needs & the revitalization of the heart."

It had not worked. Nothing worked. He was confiding in some stockmen along the bar that in all probability there would never be any relief, when a fight erupted out in the roadway and the rangemen fled out front to watch, leaving the barman sitting on his high stool behind the bar.

Ellis Bowman could not see enough of the north roadway to glimpse the battle because of the thick log abutments on each side of his window, but he was familiar with the sounds that went with it, right up to the time Marshal Thompson waded in bellowing like a bay steer.

Both the battlers were rangeriders, both were spare, weathered men in their late twenties or early thirties, and the one who in his unreasoning fury took a wild swing at Marshal Thompson had a long time to regret the inaccuracy of his aim. Thompson rocked far back from the waist until the granite-like fist had sailed past, then snapped forward.

He hit the cowboy in his stomach. The blow did not travel far but it resulted in the cowboy making terrible sounds in his throat as he closed both arms across his middle and sank to his knees.

Thompson turned on the other man, who was staring in disbelief at his adversary. His expression showed clearly that he was having trouble believing that a man could be hurt that badly by a blow that had not traveled two feet. Then Will Thompson came at him.

The cowboy darted back, then sidewards, rawboned wide shoulders curved and scarred fists poised. He was dark with a mean expression.

There were onlookers, a thin trickle of them, all male, on both sides of the wide, dusty roadway. This contest did not inspire in the onlookers the same shouting encouragement the other fight had caused. Perhaps because those were townsmen and over a period of about eight years they had seen this identical scene enacted quite often, and usually on a Saturday, with a predictable result.

Marshal Thompson had no particular talent. He had, of course, learned quite a bit about hand-fighting in his lifetime, but his power was in his size and strength. He could smother the blows of most men with his bulk, but this time he was up against a man with a faint sprinkle of gray above his ears, cold black little eyes under a protruding ridge of forehead, who was about the marshal's height but much lighter, leaner, and faster. He stung Thompson, always aiming at the face. He was fast. Each time the lawman bored in the dark cowboy dodged sideways, and in the abrupt, deep silence he cut the marshal's cheek and faded below a furious swing, stabbed Thompson twice in the area of the belt-buckle, and got away.

Thompson's face showed fury. He seemed to be carrying the fight to the cowboy, but he was also backing him toward the plankwalk while keeping the lean man busy swaying clear of smashing strikes. Only when the cowboy's heels touched the raised edge of the plankwalk did it dawn on him that he was in trouble. He tried to slide sideways without pausing to step up onto the walk, and when he shifted to raise one foot, he was off-balance. That was when Marshal Thompson charged. He hit the cowboy, making him twist to one side, then hit him again as he was staggering for balance. The third time the lawman bulled directly forward and with a roundhouse right fist, caught the rangeman alongside the head, dropping him like a pole-axed steer.

There was not a sound.

Thompson settled back, breathed deeply several times, then stepped forward, grasped the unconscious man's shirt, and when the cloth tore, he got a better grip on both ankles and literally dragged the inert man on a diagonal course across the road in plain sight of spectators, bumped him up over the boardwalk and inside the jailhouse.

He roughly rolled the cowboy over, lifted him bodily, flung his holstered Colt on the desk, and carried him like a sack of grain down into the cell-room, dumped him on the stone floor of the cell opposite Ellis Bowman's, slammed the door, locked it and without even looking around, stamped back up to the office.

Thompson was still fighting mad. Not until he had washed the cut on his cheekbone, stopped the bleeding, got his breath back and drank water from a suspended clay olla near the gunrack, was he ready to return to the roadway.

By then the first man he had knocked to his knees was no longer in town, neither were his friends, and on both sides of the roadway small groups of men stood in solemn conversation. Heads turned, eyes followed the marshal's course in the direction of the saloon, but not a word was said to him.

He had effectively dampened the holiday spirit which had prevailed before the fights in the sunbright morning.

Bowman noticed the difference; there was much less yelling back and forth. From his little window he could see stockmen leaving town with their laden wagons when normally they might have waited until late afternoon to depart.

The beaten man across the dingy corridor groaned and tried to lift himself to roll over. He failed and sank back. He had blood caked in his black hair and a discolored swelling on one side of his face. Ellis thought he was either part Indian or part Mexican. He had thin features, nostrils that flared, small sunken eyes and a wide, nearly lipless mouth. His hands, too, were swelling as he eventually pushed up into a sitting position and rolled his eyes around until they met the gaze of Ellis Bowman. It was a long time before the man got his feet and legs positioned, and pushed upright. He nearly fell, but reached the bunk, and wilted on the edge of it. After a few moments he groped with one hand up where his hair was matted, looked at the blood on his fingers and turned.

"I should have shot him," he said to Ellis.

Bowman leaned on the front of his cell saying nothing. He watched the lanky, dark man finally stand up and wince as pain seared his middle. The man sat down again and this time when he regarded the other prisoner he wagged his head slightly.

"That son of a bitch can hit. How long was I lyin' on the floor?"

"Maybe fifteen minutes. What started it?"

"Some feller hurried up over at the rack out front of the saloon and got the place I was aimin' for. I called him. We just barely got started when that town marshal come up. I think I was whipping him. I cut his face and was markin' him a little, then he come at me like a bull." The cowboy arose, looked at his bruised hands and leaned on the front of his cell. "You had any trouble with him?"

"Not your kind, no."

"If you do, friend, don't let him get anywhere near."

Ellis nodded. "What's your name?"

"Bill Morgan. What's yours?"

"Ellis Bowman. You work around here?"

"No. I been askin' around but mostly the riding crews has been filled up for a month . . . You?"

"Just came into the country."

Bill Morgan accepted that, worked his swollen hands gingerly and let go a rattling big sigh. "Gawddamn. When I struck camp this morning I figured to eat at the cafe, buy a bottle for the road and head on south." He was briefly glum, no doubt occupied with his own troubles, and then his head came up. "What did you do to get locked in here?"

"Nothing. I just rode in day before yesterday. The marshal rousted me out of my bedroll in the mountains, accused me of robbing the Batesville bank, and here I am."

Morgan seemed to be considering this because he was quiet for a while, then he raised a hand to the swelling on the side of his head as he spoke again. "You didn't rob it?"

"Rob it? I've never seen this town before he locked me in here. I didn't even know there was a town down here. No, I didn't rob it, and as long as that big tub of lard goes around settling dogfights in town, he's not going to catch whoever did rob his damned bank." Ellis shifted position on the front of his cell, watched the rawboned breed lean over to lift a trouser leg and vigorously scratch, and caught his breath. Clearly visible was the flattened bone handle of a bootknife, the kind where the scabbard was sewn inside the boot-upper.

As Morgan finished scratching Ellis said, "Didn't the marshal go over you?"

The breed wagged his head and smiled wolfishly. "I guess he was too mad to see straight."

"You better hide that thing. Sure as hell he'll be along, and

I have an idea that if he finds it on you, what happened out in the roadway might be a Sunday-school picnic."

Bill Morgan leaned, pulled out the wicked-bladed Mexican knife and looked around. There was no place to hide anything in his cell. Putting it under the straw-filled long flour sack that served as a mattress would not do because beneath it the rope springs were at least eight inches apart. Anything cached under there would fall through to the floor.

Morgan evidently was a man who could think fast in emergencies. He looked across the dingy corridor. "Did he turn you inside out?"

Ellis nodded sardonically. Morgan would probably never know how thoroughly.

The lanky breed knelt with a grimace and without another word slid his bootknife across the corridor and into Bowman's cell. It stopped moving about three feet inside and Ellis looked at it, then back at the other prisoner, who was standing up again wearing that wolfish grin. "He ain't going to search you again if he already done that, but he damned well might search me. Afterwards you can slide it back."

It was sound logic, perhaps even experienced logic, Ellis Bowman never knew which. But ten minutes later Marshal Thompson came down the corridor, opened Morgan's cell and jerked his head for the cowboy to walk ahead of him up to the office.

Morgan threw Ellis a sidelong wink and marched away. In the office Marshal Thompson had Morgan's hat from the roadway and his gun on the edge of the desk. He had shucked out every load from the old sixgun and pointed at it as he said, "Put it in your holster, and don't get clever because it's not loaded. Put the hat on too. Now you listen to me, cowboy—don't let me ever see you in my town again. You understand?"

Morgan holstered his weapon and was reaching for his hat as he bobbed his head up and down, then stood facing the larger man. "That's all?"

"No. One more thing. How much money you got?"

The breed's gaze turned dour. "Six dollars."

"Put it on the desk. That's your fine. *Put it on the desk!*"

Morgan obeyed, his features showing bitterness, but he said nothing as he emptied his pocket.

Marshal Thompson's right cheek was swollen where it had been cut in their fight, and that was the only satisfaction Bill Morgan ever got for riding into Batesville for breakfast and a bottle for the trail.

Thompson went over to the roadway door, opened it, pointed to a bay horse at the rack and said, "Get on him, and remember what I said: Don't you ever come back. Don't you even think about coming back. Now get!"

The breed hastened out to his bay horse, released the reins, snugged up the cinch, and paused briefly to gaze across his saddle-seat at the town marshal. Then he smiled, swung up, and without a word or even a glance back at the jailhouse, rode past the cafe, past the general store, past the blacksmith's shop and kept on riding south until he was a speck in the sunbright distance.

Marshal Thompson pocketed the six dollars and went after some salve over at the apothecary's shop for his split cheek, then had a clear sidewalk all the way up to the saloon where he spent ten cents of Bill Morgan's money for a glass of tepid beer.

He had figured everything out. He had already told Bowman he had been three thousand dollars short of the money from the bank.

The beer was refreshing. He drained half the glass.

Now, he would take Bowman back up into the Custer Meadow country to look for the missing three thousand dollars, which he would accuse Bowman of having cached up there—then he would shoot him, roll him down a canyon where he'd never be found, and return to town. As far as anyone in town would know, he had turned Bowman loose because he hadn't been the bank robber after all.

He finished the glass and banged the bartop for a refill. While he was waiting he considered his purple cheek, and smiled. Charley Turner had said that was not bank money. He had also said Will was holding an innocent man.

Thompson was still smiling when the barman returned with his glass. Any time he could make twelve thousand dollars, plus another six dollars, in just one day, was maybe one of the best strokes of luck of his lifetime, no matter what happened afterwards.

The barman, emboldened by the marshal's smile, said, "You sure put those two men down in a hurry, Will."

Thompson continued to smile as he enclosed the glass in a huge fist. "That's what the town council pays me for. Keep order and cracks heads if I got to, to do it . . . This is good beer."

"Mister Wheeler just bottled it last week. He got old Jed Cuthbert to send off back east somewhere for regular brewer's yeast and hops. I'll tell him you liked it. That'll please him and lately the way his feet's been painin' him, I think he can use somethin' to make him smile a little."

# CHAPTER 5
## Facing a Deadly Fact

ELLIS Bowman had never carried a bootknife. Nor was there a sewn scabbard inside his right boot and when he eased the knife out of sight down there, the point drew blood so he had to remove the weapon, wrap it with his handkerchief, and see whether he could walk without cutting himself. He took a few steps until he was satisfied.

By the time the marshal brought his supper Ellis was as hungry as a bitchwolf. Also by that time, except for John Wheeler's saloon The Waterhole, Batesville was quiet; merchants were glad for the opportunity to lock up for the day and go home. Otherwise, townsfolk were thinking about supper. The stockmen who had lingered filled the cadaverous man's counter over at the cafe, and whoever had been shaping steel over an anvil had stopped doing that too.

Tomorrow, about seven o'clock, someone would ring the church bell but otherwise Batesville would be as orderly on Sunday as it had not been on Saturday, and that also was how things were west of the Missouri River.

The banker met Marshal Thompson in front of the apothecary's shop and brought up the subject of the stolen money. "You've got the wrong man in that cell," Charley Turner concluded. "Could be so," Thompson agreed, grinning wolfishly.

Charley Turner eyed the lawman thoughtfully and a little warily when he also said, "There's a good chance the bank will have to close unless we get that money back."

Because Thompson thought that was a reproach and was stung by it, he answered curtly. "Charley, there was more

**33**

than your damned eleven thousand right there in your hands when you counted it. If you an' your clerk say it ain't the same money, why then all I can do is turn my prisoner loose an' about all you can do is set down and cry." Thompson checked his annoyance. "But I'll put out a dodger on the bank robber."

Turner nodded gravely, knowing as well as Marshal Thompson that printing and distributing a wanted poster on someone with eleven thousand dollars in cash in his saddle-bags, even if it got back the thief for Batesville, was not at all likely to get the money back.

Will Thompson was eyeing the forlorn face of the banker when he said something else. "Charley, you had the eleven thousand."

"It wasn't the bank's money, Will."

Thompson's brown eyes glowed sardonically. "Money is money. You had your chance . . . I got to go now."

Charles Turner stood watching the large man cross the road. This was not the first time in eight years that he'd had reason to suspect Will Thompson's ethics might be nonexistent. He headed for home with some unhappy thoughts.

Thompson made a pot of coffee in his office, washed his face, salved it again, dug a plug of Kentucky Twist from a shirt pocket and settled a bittersweet cud into his cheek before taking a cup of java back to the desk with him.

Twelve thousand dollars—shy a few dollars though not very many—was a damned fortune. Why, a man could buy a ranch with that kind of money, or maybe half interest in a successful saloon with a card room. Or he could just sit back and live extremely well while the world went limping along on its miserable way.

He finished the coffee and went down into the cell-room. His prisoner was sleeping. Marshal Thompson rattled the door. "Bowman! Wake up! You and I are goin' ridin' in the morning. Back up near that old shack where you buried part of the bank loot."

Ellis swung his legs over the side of the bunk and perched there gazing through the steel straps. "What time tomorrow?"

"What's the difference? Time don't mean anythin' to someone in your fix . . . Before sunup in the morning, Bowman, because I want to be back in town before dusk."

Ellis dropped his head slightly to regard the scuffed toes of his boots. He very quietly said, "Marshal, up at the Hanks cabin you said all the bank money was in my belt. Those possemen heard you say it . . . There is no shortage."

Thompson, who did not remember what he had said up on Custer Meadow, gazed malevolently at his prisoner. "I'm not very good at figuring." Having said that, Will Thompson stood eyeing Ellis Bowman. "It was the banker counting the money with me that come up with three thousand bein' short."

Ellis continued to sit on the edge of his bunk for a long while without speaking or looking up. When it seemed he might never speak he said, "There's something I didn't tell you up at that cabin. I saw the feller who owns that sorrel horse up in the timber behind the cabin down on his knees digging."

Ellis raised his head. Marshal Thompson was staring at him. After a moment he said, "Well, we'll ride up there tomorrow an' you can show me where he was doing that."

Thompson turned and went back up to his office leaving Ellis Bowman listening to his diminishing footfalls before he dropped back on the cot staring at the ceiling.

He had lied. That appeared to be normal for the relationship he had with Marshal Thompson, and he was certain Thompson had lied to him, not once but at least twice, the first time when he said there was a shortage in the money stolen from the bank, and the second time when he had said they would ride up to Custer Meadow because he thought the money was hidden there. He didn't think any such thing.

Thompson knew there was no shortage. At the shack he had said that Ellis' moneybelt carried the full amount robbed from the Batesville bank, plus a little more.

Then why was he going to take Ellis back up into the mountains? For twelve thousand damned dollars that had nothing to do with the bank, but which had everything to do with Ellis Bowman. In short Thompson was going to kill him up there, cache his body, and ride back to take possession of Bowman's moneybelt.

Ellis arose, paced restlessly, wiggled his right ankle inside its boot to reassure himself of the knife he was concealing, and finally stepped onto the stool to look out the narrow long window. What he saw upon the far plankwalk was Marshal Thompson in conversation with that bull-built, badly weathered man who had been one of the posse up at Custer Meadow. At the time of his capture that had been the man who had held the false mustache on his gloved palm, and who later pointed to Ellis's middle and suggested to the lawman that he make Ellis shed his shirt.

He had not paid any particular attention to the man at the time of his capture nor on the ride down to the Batesville jailhouse, but now he made a particular study.

Whoever that short, massively muscled older man was, he and Marshal Thompson were obviously more than just a lawman and someone he had dragooned to be a posseman. They were standing and talking like old friends.

Ellis got down off the stool, went to the front of his cell and gripped the cold steel straps. Hell! Thompson would not have to miss supper tomorrow. In fact he would not even have to go into the mountains if he had a partner. The marshal could kill him when they were far enough from town for the echo of the gunshot not to carry—even if anyone would be listening about four o'clock in the morning—hand over the reins of the sorrel horse to that bull-necked older man who would then take the corpse and the horse deep into the mountains, shoot the horse and roll them both down into a damned dark, deep canyon.

It was not necessary to leave Batesville in the dark in order to reach Custer Meadow and return before dusk. It had not taken that long to ride down from there the day Thompson had brought him in.

The marshal had lied about that too; he wanted to leave town with Bowman when it was dark, with people still abed, so that he would not be seen riding out with his prisoner.

Ellis returned to the bunk and sank down upon the edge of it as darkness came closer. He heard the roadside door open and close, a muted sound because of the thickness of the cell-room door. Once, he thought he heard a man's voice raised in anger but although he went to the front of the cell to listen, he did not hear anything like that again.

Thompson came along to light the coal oil lamp and hang it from its hook in the ceiling of the corridor. The glass mantle had not been cleaned in ages, nor had the wick been trimmed which resulted in the lamp smoking badly, further darkening the glass.

As Thompson settled back from this chore he turned and asked, "Where did you say you come from up in Wyoming?"

"A town called Runnymede."

Thompson nodded. "Who'd you leave behind up there?"

"No one."

"No folks, no cousins, no one?"

Ellis stared out past the steel straps. It was too late to invent a fictitious relative who might come hunting for him down into the Custer Meadow and Batesville country. "No cousins, no one at all. Some friends." Ellis shrugged. "I was an orphan."

"An orphan?" The big lawman's brows lifted slightly. "Is that a fact? Well now, we got that in common. Me, someone left me in a basket on an old widow-woman's doorstep back in Nebraska."

"She raised you?"

Thompson's brown eyes glittered. "Not exactly. She put me to work walkin' barefoot in washtubs eight, ten hours a day when I was no more'n four. When I was nine she hired me out to a horsetrader who mumbled an' because I couldn't understand him and asked what he said, he'd beat hell out of me with a harness tug."

Ellis wagged his head. "How old were you when you got away from them?"

"Twelve. I took them both wagon-ridin' to see some silver-lookin' rocks and when we got the hell and gone into some trees and underbrush, I hanged 'em both."

Bowman was stunned by the marshal's admission. Then he saw Thompson's devilish grin and thought the marshal was pulling his leg. Either that or he was the most cold-blooded killer Bowman had ever met.

Thompson leaned on the cell bars. "How about you, bein' an orphan?"

"It wasn't too bad. My folks died during an epidemic at Council Bluffs and a preacher and his wife took me in. They were good folks. I left them when I was fifteen and began hiring out." Ellis looked into the slightly swollen, coarse face of the larger man. "I could use a drink of water."

Thompson continued to lean a while, then departed. Fifteen minutes later he returned with a coffee tin full of water and since it was too tall to slide under the door, he unlocked the padlock and handed the can to Bowman, cold brown eyes fixed on his prisoner the way a rattlesnake stares at a baby bird.

After the lawman returned to his office Ellis put the water can aside and stepped back onto the milking stool, but darkness was settling fast. All he could see was reflected lamplight upon the window of the general store.

Someone was playing a piano, two men called to one another and a light rig with yellow wheels and tassels along the top passed at a slow walk. Reflected light shone off the face of a lithe, handsome woman whose waves of fair hair framed a cameo-like face. He stared, and for no reason she turned her head in his direction just before the buggy-mare pulled the rig out of sight. Ellis stepped down a little unsteadily to the floor of his cell, turned and said, "Gawd almighty—she looks like Sam Hanks!"

He did not even hear Marshal Thompson slam the roadside door and roughly padlock it from the outside.

# CHAPTER 6
# Toward the Meadow

THE next morning Ellis considered whether he should tell the marshal about the woman. She must be related to the man he'd known as Sam Hanks, maybe even his twin. But he decided to hold his peace for awhile; if he was right about Thompson being ruthless, the marshal would kill him for his money anyway. If he was wrong, the marshal would let him go regardless of the whereabouts of this so-called Sam Hanks.

Ellis was awake and ready when Marshal Thompson came down into the cell-room, opened the cell door and jerked his head. Up in the jailhouse office Thompson handed Bowman a cup of black coffee. He did not say a word to his prisoner until he had drained his cup and was refilling it. The office lamp did not smoke and the wick had been trimmed but it still gave off a minimum of light. Outside, the world was dark, silent and chilly.

"You could use a shave, Bowman. Most likely a bath, to boot."

Ellis neither responded nor looked at the marshal. The coffee preoccupied him. It was as bitter as tanning acid but it was hot, and since it was probably all he was going to put into his stomach for a long time, he made it last.

As he was finishing the coffee he said, "What I need, Marshal, is my moneybelt back, and five hundred miles between this town and somewhere else."

Thompson put both cups on a shelf near the wallrack of weapons, went to the door where a booted Winchester had recently been positioned, picked it up, hung it in the crook of one arm and jerked his head. "South to the corral out

**40**

behind the liverybarn. I got the horses rigged out an' tied down there."

As Ellis stepped out into the chill he said, "You been busy, this morning."

They cut through a refuse-littered empty piece of ground between two small stores to reach the alley, then went down it to the corral stringer where the sorrel was tethered beside a large brown horse with powerful legs, a wide chest, and a roached mane.

Thompson did not take his eyes off Bowman as he buckled the saddlegun boot under his right *rosadero*, tested the cinch by rocking the saddle by its horn, then said, "Get up there and turn back up the alley. When we reach the end of town we can slant northwest and lope a few miles."

Ellis did as he had been told. When they were well away from Batesville he slackened a little to examine as much of the countryside as he could make out in semidarkness. He had been through here once before, on the ride to Batesville as Marshal Thompson's prisoner. But there were not many landmarks he could distinguish until false dawn arrived with its pewter light and deathly silence.

They were far enough from town now for the murder to take place. Ellis spat and eyed his large companion. The reason he had taken so long last night to respond to Marshal Thompson back in the cell was because he had been working out an idea that would save his life at least until he could reach Custer Meadow. Thompson had taken Ellis's bait hook, line and sinker.

Ellis had not seen anyone on his knees behind the cabin, but as long as Marshal Thompson believed someone had buried something valuable there, he would not kill the man who could show him the spot where the digging had taken place.

As he considered Thompson now, and smiled, Ellis knew that once they got up to Custer Meadow he was going to have to come up with another idea; but for the time being he felt safe. Wherever that weathered, short man with the bull-neck was hiding with his Winchester, Ellis was reasonably sure of his safety—until after sunrise anyway.

Thompson got a chew of tobacco into his cheek and offered the plug. Ellis shook his head. Thompson said, almost amiably, "What did you figure to do with that money; maybe open a liverybarn somewhere?"

"No. I didn't have any plans. Just ride until I found a place where it didn't come up with a black frost every blessed morning for nine months out of the year. After I found it, why then I'd think about what to do."

"That's a lot of money to be ridin' around with," stated Marshal Thompson, and got a long, hard look from his companion, who thought that the marshal, whether he realized it or not, had just revealed that he knew the money had not come from a bank robbery.

"Yeah, maybe, but most of the time I was back in the mountains where there wasn't another human being. It was safe enough."

Thompson mentioned something that had been bothering him faintly but persistently for a week. Sam Hanks. "There ain't no Sam Hanks, Bowman. There hasn't been in five, maybe six years . . . How'd you come up with that name, bein' plumb new to the country?"

Bowman's reply was so long in coming Marshal Thompson scowled at him. The reason for this delay was his vivid recollection of that young woman in the top-buggy last evening. It had been almost the same face—without the mustache and the mass of sorrel-blond hair stuffed inside an old hat—just as surely as Ellis was living and breathing. He would willingly have wagered all his earthly possessions, including his belt full of money, that the woman he saw last night could lead him to a Sam Hanks who was very much alive.

He said, "I told you the truth, Marshal. He was at the

shack. This sorrel horse belongs to him. My horse is a bay ridgling with my initials on his left shoulder."

The large man reached with one gloved hand to lightly rub the tip of his nose. He seemed more baffled than anything else. As he lowered his hand to the saddle-swell he said, "It just plain couldn't have been. Did he have a full beard, all white?"

"Clean-shaven except for that mustache an' I guess that was just stuck on his face."

"Old?"

"No. My guess would be twenty to twenty-five."

Thompson's bafflement seemed to deepen and for a mile or so he said no more, but as they were entering the foothills with the timbered slopes dead ahead, he finally spoke again. "It wasn't old Sam Hanks, for a damned fact, so it had to be someone using his name."

Ellis Bowman, who had already arrived at this same conclusion, said, "All right. Whoever he was, Marshal, he is your bank robber. I'm not."

Thompson scowled at his horse's ears. He knew two facts about this affair, and he had no intention of commenting on either of them. He knew, because Charley Turner had convinced him of it, that Ellis Bowman had not been carrying the bank money. The other thing he knew was that since Bowman had not been carrying the bank money, he had not robbed the damned bank. Then who the hell *had* robbed it?

His brow cleared as they entered the country around on the west side of the immense barranca which was Custer Meadow in gray pre-dawn light. If whoever had robbed the bank had stolen Bowman's horse and left him to be caught by possemen, then it was likely that he had indeed buried his loot up in the timber atop the meadow. That would make Will Thompson a rich man if it was all there, and if he found it, because then he would have twice the amount of money he now considered as his own.

Will Thompson was one of those physically forceful individuals who was not capable of lengthy reasoning. Twelve thousand dollars and a dead man made good sense to him. Eleven thousand more, even if it was crisp new money, not unheard of, and even if he could not spend it within miles of the Batesville bank, was even better. He totalled it as he followed the sorrel horse up the rather steep, wide trail to the meadow, and came up with something like twenty-two or twenty-three thousand dollars; more money than he had ever seen at one time in his life, or had ever imagined he might own. Everything he had ever wanted to own he could buy with that kind of wealth, or he could just go out to some place like San Francisco's Barbary Coast and never have to work again as long as he lived.

Bowman's voice brought Thompson back to the present with abrupt suddenness. "Do you expect Sam Hanks buried the entire eleven thousand from the bank up here?"

Thompson wanted to believe it. "Likely. One thing he could damn well count on—I'd be after him. He had to run for it."

"It was paper money, wasn't it? Then why not take it along? Paper money don't weigh much."

"I got no idea, but I can tell you from experience that outlaws do damned fool things."

Ellis agreed, then said, "Yeah. Marshal, I've been thinking. If I lead you to his cache and all the bank money is there—I want my money back and long headstart out of your territory."

Will Thompson's brown eyes narrowed against Bowman's back. Without any hesitation he said, "All right. Tonight when we get back."

Ellis, who was up ahead facing forward, smiled bleakly to himself.

They reached the topout and paused. Blue sky lit the east. The shadowy terrain took on form in the light of the new day. The beauty, insularity, serenity of this immense grassland meadow touched Bowman as it had before. Only this time he viewed it as something familiar—and worth acquiring. It possessed everything a stockman could want. Miles of graze and browse, shade, timber, water, and it was on the south slope which was where sunshine always arrived first in summer or winter.

As the horses were catching their breath from the climb, he asked Marshal Thompson who owned Custer Meadow. The big man spat amber, shrugged and replied with indifference. "Damned if I know. Old Sam Hanks used to own it."

"All of it?"

"Yeah, and back up northward through the timber for some distance. But now, maybe no one owns it. He didn't leave no children as far as I know. The lower-down stockmen used to graze it off during early spring and summer, but it was too far to drive critters, and there's bears and cougars and whatnot back in them mountains . . . They quit coming up here a few years back . . . . Let's move out."

They rode for an hour through timber that formed a wedge-shaped area of deep, fragrant shade, then emerged within sight of the old log house. There was a sow bear with two cubs at the cabin. The men heard them before they rode closer and saw the cubs playing at ripping up the rotten old porch boards in their search for rodents or grubs while the old sow explored the cabin's interior.

Ellis halted, rested both hands atop the saddlehorn and said, "She's going to be touchy, Marshal."

Thompson leaned to draw his Winchester from beneath his leg. "Not for long she ain't going to be."

"If you shoot her and her cubs, and there's an old boar bear back in the trees somewhere, we're likely not to get back to Batesville until long after dark—maybe not until tomorrow."

Thompson still sat forward with a hand on the butt of his carbine glaring up where the cubs were flinging rotten wood in several directions. He finally leaned back, took his hand away from the carbine stock and sat watching as the sow finally emerged, raised her head to sniff, walked through the wreckage her cubs had made, and stopped dead-still in the early slanting sunshine about twenty feet from the cabin, to move her raised head from side to side, and occasionally up and down. She had a scent.

Thompson and Bowman sat motionless. The sow did not have their scent because she was interested in something east of the cabin. When she finally reared up on her hind legs trying to see the object of her interest with her poor eyesight, Ellis gazed that way too.

So that was where the marshal's friend with the weathered, badly checked and lined face, was waiting.

Marshal Thompson growled. "She'll hang around all day."

He might have been correct if the sow had not abandoned her interest in whatever was out of sight in the tall grass or in one of the spits of timber that came down onto the meadow, and turned to round up her cubs.

Whatever had upset her was a threat. Ellis could see that from the protective way she cuffed the cubs away from the house, and continued to cuff them as she hurriedly herded them northward into the timber.

Ellis watched that distant country where whatever had made the sow bear anxious was located, and did not see anything. Not even a deer or a circling bird.

"Let's get up there," he said.

Their horses, though, were a lot less than anxious. Bear scent was strong enough for the men to smell it. Horses with an aversion to bears and far superior smelling ability had the full, rank, carrion-tainted gamey stench in their nostrils and refused to go closer to the cabin than about three hundred feet.

Will Thompson raked his big horse with spur rowels. In response he got the promise of a fight. Ellis said, "He's not going up there. You hook him a few more times and he's going to stick your head in the ground."

Thompson's anger was transferred from his horse to his

two-legged companion. "He'll go if I got to skin him alive, an' you keep out of it."

Ellis was calm in the face of the lawman's frustration. "If he dumps you up here and gets away—it'll be a hell of a long walk back. If you're able to walk." As he said this Ellis swung to the ground and led his wild-eyed mount over to the nearest tree and tethered it. When he turned, Marshal Thompson was on the ground too, still mad as a hornet, yanking his big brown horse over to also be tied. He pulled out the carbine, swore at the frightened big horse then turned on Bowman again. "You stay ahead of me, an' you better remember your manners!"

Ellis approached the old cabin far enough to one side to be able to see the northward timber, up where that sow bear had herded her cubs. If she had plenty of room to maneuver, did not feel pressed nor threatened, she would probably keep on going, but if there was one completely unpredictable creature on God's green earth, it was a sow bear with cubs. Neither men nor guns, not even a buzz-saw, would prevent a bear in a rage from attacking.

The smell was especially rank at the cabin because there was not a breath of air stirring, and the bears had not been gone more than a few minutes. Ellis stepped carefully through the debris left behind by the grub-hunting cubs and entered the cabin with Marshal Thompson close behind.

The sow had not done much damage. Except for tearing off a cupboard door and scattering flour, baking soda, and coffee on the floor, she had evidently decided there was nothing worth eating or carrying away before she had come outside.

Marshal Thompson stood with the Winchester in the crook of one arm staring at the spilled flour and coffee. He looked baffled again. "Was that your grub?"

"No. It was in the cupboard when I found the cabin." Ellis watched the lawman's coarse features. "I figured it belonged to Sam Hanks."

Marshal Thompson's brown eyes came up showing anger. "Sam Hanks! That wasn't Sam Hanks! There's no way it could have been, and besides your description wouldn't have fit old Hanks."

Ellis shrugged. "All right, it wasn't. But it was someone, and that flour and coffee belonged to him."

Marshal Thompson looked elsewhere in the shadowy room, then settled his gaze upon Ellis Bowman. "We're wastin' time. That damned bear made things worse. I told you—I want to get back to town. Now then, walk out of here and up yonder where you saw that man digging."

# CHAPTER 7
# The Pointed Gun

ELLIS went out to the mouldy devastation of the porch and paused. Everything had led up to this moment. He had only a boot-knife he could not draw rapidly while behind him was the big lawman with a carbine and a sixgun.

Thompson prodded him with the Winchester barrel. "What are you waiting for?"

Ellis half turned as he replied, "I thought I heard a horse nicker off there somewhere to the east."

Thompson dug him in the back again. "Move along. I told you before I ain't got all day."

The distance from the cabin to the first rank of trees was several hundred yards. Ellis walked without haste and without seeming to be hanging back. He could prolong this walk just so long, and he could do the same by pretending to be looking for the exact spot he had seen a man on his knees digging into the ground, but what was as certain as night followed day was that within the next hour he would live or die. With that in mind, the hidden knife seemed an awfully long way from his hand, and the possibility of successfully attacking a very large armed man—even if he could get at the knife—was not very great.

He paused once. "Did you hear that? I think the sow's still around."

Thompson gouged Bowman in the back again, more savagely this time. "You leave the sow to me. You just keep walking."

The second time Bowman halted, less than two hundred feet from the timber, they both heard a horse whinny some-

49

where to the east. Thompson ignored the sound. "You stop one more time an' I'm going to brain you."

Ellis reached shade and fragrance and paused beside an immense red fir to look back. Unless Marshal Thompson had known there was a horse to the east somewhere, he would certainly have acted with at least surprise. The fact that he was not surprised, and did not give a damn, was about all the proof Bowman needed to understand that Thompson's friend was indeed up here and lying in wait.

They were among trees of great size and age where sunlight only penetrated in cathedral-like slanting shafts, and there was a lingering touch of ancient dust stirred to life by the sow bear and her cubs.

The ground was marked in all directions where small animals, and some that were not so small, had rooted and dug. Ellis began a sashaying walk as he said, "In here somewhere."

Will Thompson slung the Winchester in the crook of one arm and began a slow, methodical search for something that would appear as freshly disturbed earth. After several minutes he said, "Where exactly did you see him digging?"

Ellis shook his head. "All these damned trees look alike. It's around here somewhere."

As they resumed their shuffling search Thompson muttered, "It sure as hell better be." He was sweating and it was not that warm among the forest giants. Twice he used the tip of his Winchester to stir in soft places and the third time he did this he said, "Bowman! Look over here!"

Ellis walked over. There was a low mound that seemed to have been pressed flat. Without a word he sank to his knees with the Batesville marshal standing to one side and watching as he scooped earth. It was a moment of intense concentration for Thompson. Ellis feigned the same anxiety when from the corner of his eye he caught a shadow of movement. At about the same moment a stocky man with faded trousers and shirt darted from behind a tree and leveled a sixgun.

Ellis saw him first, recognized the weather-battered, deeply lined face and thick neck. Only when Ellis rocked back and stopped digging did Marshal Thompson straighten up as though to snarl curses—and also saw the man holding the sixgun.

Ellis heard Thompson's sudden intake of breath. Five seconds later the weathered man said, "Drop the rifle, Will."

Thompson got livid. "Jake, what in the hell . . . You was supposed to be out yonder waiting for him to ride in front of you on the way back."

"Drop the Winchester," the short man said again, in a voice that sounded to Ellis Bowman more strained than threatening. "Drop it you damned fool!"

Those last five words had sounded desperate. Ellis looked straight at the faded man. He had the sixgun barrel directly in front with the bullet cylinder showing on each side of the barrel.

*There were no bullets in the cylinder!*

"Will, you're goin' to get yourself killed if you don't let go of that Winchester."

Thompson was stiff with outrage but he let the saddlegun fall to the spongy ground. Then he swore. "You double-crossin' son of a bitch!"

The faded man licked his lips and wigwagged with his unloaded gun. "Now the Colt," he said. Ellis looked up at Marshal Thompson. He was too tall and probably too angry to have noticed, even if he could have seen down into the sixgun cylinder, that there were no bullets in it.

"Jake, I'm goin' to kill you if it's the last thing I ever do."

"Drop the sixgun, Will. That's the last time I'm goin' to tell you."

Instead of obeying, Marshal Thompson wagged with one arm in the direction of the hole Ellis had dug. "It's not there. Look for yourself. We ain't found it yet." Thompson stopped gesturing to stare at his confederate. "You darned fool, you jumped us too soon. We don't have it yet."

"Will—you drop that gun or so help me . . . !"

Ellis spoke softly. "You better do it, Marshal. At that distance a blind man could hit the eye of a needle."

Thompson reluctantly lowered his right hand very slowly, closed his fingers around the walnut stock of his weapon, and the short man said, "Two fingers, Will. You're lookin' death right in the eye. Just two fingers now."

Thompson obeyed. His weapon fell within eighteen inches of Ellis Bowman's right hand. Ellis was coming to a decision about the gun. He knew it was loaded. He knew the bull-necked man's gun was not loaded. He could shoot the short man without risking anything, then he could shoot Marshal Thompson before the big man could grab his fallen Winchester.

He moved his right hand—and a knife-edged tenor voice spoke from behind the huge red-barked old fir tree where Jake was standing. "Don't move, cowboy. Don't touch that gun."

Ellis looked up. Will Thompson was staring. The man called Jake had sweat beads on his upper lip and forehead, and he did not take his eyes off Marshal Thompson as the second handgun appeared, cocked and definitely loaded in the gloved hand of the same individual Ellis had encountered in the cabin a week earlier. The gun-holder was wearing the same big old loose coat, battered hat, faded trousers and cracked old boots. But this time there was a blue bandana across the tanned face reaching from the bridge of the nose to the throat.

Marshal Thompson's eyes were bulging. Ellis spoke into the deathly silence. "Marshal, that's Sam Hanks."

Sam Hanks ignored Ellis except to order him to get back to his feet. Hanks's attention was fixed on the large man with the badge on his shirt. "Sit down," he said. When Thompson acted deaf the cocked sixgun tipped upward in the direction of his face. "Sit down!"

Thompson grunted as he got down into a squatting posture. He was staring at Sam Hanks with what appeared to be a struggling realization of some kind.

Sam Hanks tossed a pigging string to Ellis Bowman. "Tie his arms in back. Use his belt for his ankles, and if he tries to kick you I'll kill him . . . Jake, you too, sit down."

Jake did not hesitate.

When Ellis had finished with the marshal and stood up, the gunman nodded toward Jake. "The same. You'll have to use his belts. That's the only length of rope I have."

As Ellis moved toward Jake the short man looked imploringly at Will Thompson and bleated. "I couldn't do nothin' else, Will. He come up behind me. I was watchin' you and Bowman cross from the trees to the shack after that bear went away. I didn't hear a blessed thing. He put his gunbarrel against the back of my neck. I liked to have jumped out of my skin . . . He herded me over here after unloadin' my gun and we been waitin' for you to come up here. I had to do what I did, Will. He'd have shot me sure as hell if I hadn't."

Marshal Thompson did not take his eyes off Sam Hanks, not even during Jake's fearful explanation. When silence returned he said, "Who are you?"

The answer was exactly what Thompson should have expected. "Sam Hanks."

Thompson slowly wagged his head. "No. You know a damned sight better'n that. But I know you from somewhere."

The lashing of Jake's arms and ankles was more difficult because neither Jake's trouser belt nor shellbelt had holes where Ellis needed them. He got a claspknife from Jake's trouser pocket to twist holes in the leather, finished the lashing, dropped the claspknife and stood up. His expression was perfectly calm as he watched Sam Hanks ease down the hammer of his weapon and holster it. Ellis smiled at Hanks and got back a slightly surprised and annoyed look. Then Hanks stepped completely away from the big old fir tree and gazed thoughtfully at the prisoners. "Marshal, I ought to kill you. You've had it coming for eight years."

Thompson said nothing. He never once took his eyes off the half-hidden face of Sam Hanks. Jake did not look at anyone. He was sweaty and shaking.

Ellis stood waiting. It mattered not at all to him how long this confrontation might drag on. By rights he should have been dead by now. The fact that he wasn't—and the fact that he knew something neither Thompson nor his friend knew—pleased and amused him.

Sam Hanks said, "Mister Bowman, why did he bring you back up here?"

Ellis eyed Sam Hanks pensively. "If you don't know that, how come you're here?"

"Because I heard Jake telling some friends last night out front of the general store he had to ride up to Custer Meadow in the morning, right early . . . And before that I saw Jake and Marshal Thompson talking in front of the general store."

Ellis nodded slightly. "You're pretty good at putting two and two together, Sam. Where is my horse?"

Sam Hanks' right hand went to the handle of that loaded gun. "I asked you a question, Mister Bowman. Why did he bring you up here?"

"Because I lied like a trooper. I told him I saw you bury something among the trees up here, and left it to him to think you buried the loot from the bank robbery. He brought me up here to show him where you'd cached it." Ellis paused, gazing at the hat brim shadowed green eyes. "How did you know I was in the Batesville jail?"

Sam Hanks looked annoyed again. "It was no secret. Hasn't been one for a week." Hanks faced Marshal Thompson again and gave Ellis another order. "Use his handkerchief and blindfold him. Both of them."

That order had no particular visible effect upon the lawman but Jake looked frantically at Sam Hanks. "What you goin' to do? I done everything you said, didn't I? Besides, I never had no hand in anything' Will Thompson done years back. I wasn't even in the country at that —"

"Mitchell, shut up! Not another word! Blindfold him, Mister Bowman."

Ellis went to work. When he straightened up he eyed Sam Hanks with interest. With mock seriousness he said, "You want to shoot them or do you want me to do it?"

Jake bleated and strained against his bindings but Marshal Thompson neither moved nor made a sound.

Hanks said, "Get them on their feet. Remove the ankle bindings. Good. Now, Mister Bowman, get the sorrel horse and Marshal Thompson's horse. You can catch up. I'll start east with them down in the open. It's a long walk back to where I left my horse and the other one."

Ellis met the steady gaze of Sam Hanks, controlling an urge to grin.

The woman he had seen was not the sister of Sam Hanks: She *was* Sam Hanks. The stare he got back showed absolutely no trace of amusement. "What are you waiting for, Mister Bowman?"

Ellis started back in the direction of the cabin. From there it was a healthy hike to the trees where the horses had been tethered after the encounter with the sow bear and her cubs. All the way south Ellis laughed to himself. But he had a feeling that Marshal Thompson was not going to be fooled much longer. The way Thompson had been staring at Sam Hanks inclined Bowman to believe that Thompson might recognize this imposter—without the bandana, the old hat and the big old baggy coat. Eventually he was going to make the connection between the Sam Hanks who had threatened to kill him, and some young woman who was not Sam Hanks at all.

As Ellis freed the horses, mounted the sorrel and trailed the big brown horse, he speculated about Hanks' remark to

Will Thompson that he ought to shoot him. The tangents leading from such a statement were almost infinite, but of one thing Ellis felt very certain—if the marshal gave Sam Hanks a valid excuse to shoot him, Sam Hanks would do it.

# CHAPTER 8
## A Very Confusing Time

THE morning was advancing toward midday, and there was autumn heat out in the open, although in the timber a hint of late-summer chill was noticeable. As Ellis Bowman rode in the wake of the distant figures on foot, he occasionally gazed higher, where the abrupt and soundless explosion of autumn colors seemed to have arrived all at the same time. Undoubtedly there had been killing frosts up here for a week or maybe longer.

By the time he came up behind Sam Hanks driving the blindfolded captives by telling them when to move right or left, Ellis was beginning to wonder less about Sam Hanks being a woman and more about why Sam Hanks would use the name of someone who had been dead for years. He also respected the way Sam Hanks handled a gun.

When finally they reached the place where a nondescript brown horse was dozing in tree shade, Sam Hanks had a red and sweaty face. Ellis shook his head. To be comfortable all Hanks had to do was shed that knee-length old riding coat.

They halted in slanting shadows of early afternoon, and Ellis wordlessly led the nondescript seal-brown gelding down to where the prisoners were. He looked toward Hanks, who nodded. "Boost him up there, Mister Bowman. It's not far to the place where I left my horse."

Jake's shirt-front was drenched in sweat and although he was silent now, the twisting of his mouth beneath his blindfold showed his dread.

Hanks led Jake's horse to where the other horse was tied. When Ellis saw the animal he did not at first dismount. When he finally climbed down he walked over to Sam Hanks,

57

shoved the reins of the rawboned sorrel horse into a gloved hand, glared in defiance and walked up into the trees to free his ridgling and lead it back.

He did not say a word. Neither did Sam Hanks. Each of them took the reins of one of the horses carrying the captives and Sam Hanks led off again. One thing was clear: whoever Sam Hanks was, whatever motivation had created this situation, Sam knew Custer Meadow. A mile farther along where the eastern flow of the plateau seemed to abruptly drop away, except to the north where it was part of some upthrusting timbered slopes, Hanks angled slightly northward and surprised Ellis by passing through a spit of yellow pine and crossing a slick-rock ledge, then starting downward over a wide, dusty old game trail as crooked as a dog's hind leg.

Not a word was spoken. If Ellis had been able to feel sympathy for the blindfolded, trussed captives, he would have felt it as their horses began the descent. Thompson and Jake Mitchell could tell by the tip of their saddles that they were going down off Custer Meadow, but not by way of the better trail back across the plateau to the west.

A couple of times Ellis held his breath but Sam Hanks on the functional but homely sorrel horse did not even stiffen in the saddle when the sorrel had to stop, position his legs and body just right, then stretch to cross erosion gullies that cut the trail from one side to the other.

On the lefthand side as Ellis's ridgling was gingerly navigating one of these deathtraps, Ellis looked down. It was not a straight drop of several hundred feet but the barranca wall was nearly straight down. It had jagged splinters of rock protruding like swords. If a man and a horse fell, they would be slashed to shreds before they got to the flat country.

Ellis blew out a breath. There were birds flying *below* him.

Sam Hanks covered the last hundred yards sitting twisted to look back. Somewhere between the meadow and the bottom of the old trail, Sam had yanked down the blue bandana. Ellis gazed at the face he had seen briefly by pale dusk-light last night in the roadway of Batesville.

Sam faced forward, without speaking pointed eastward and led the way alongside the massive base of the plateau toward some handsome sugar pines whose height was impressive. Ellis, while perfectly willing to trail along, began to wonder just how long this damned horseback ride was going to take and where in hell it might end.

Among the towering pines, they came upon a faint trail, raised dust as they traveled along it for no more than a half mile, and emerged upon an emerald glade of perhaps sixty or seventy acres.

Sam halted, waited until Ellis arrived, then said, "Hobble the horses. They can pick grass for a while. I want to talk to you."

Ellis met Sam's green-eyed gaze intending to speak but Sam, probably in anticipation, swung to the ground and walked back beside Marshal Thompson. "Get down."

Thompson, whose mind had not been idle during their long ride, had an answer ready. "Untie my hands."

"Get down, Marshal. If you're careful you won't fall. Get down or I'll pull you down."

Ellis came over expecting the large man to fall, but Thompson managed it well enough. Ellis went back to help Jake dismount. Jake, too, had a good sense of balance and came down without stumbling, and immediately began to complain. Midway through a sentence Ellis Bowman made a leisurely reach, got a fistful of shirtcloth, pulled Jake close and softly said, "Don't open your damned mouth unless someone asks you to," and gave the older man a rough shove.

It required more time to get the prisoners settled on the ground, with their ankles lashed again so they could not run, than it did to drive the horses out where the best feed was.

On the way back from driving horses, walking side by side, Sam Hanks said, "I'm interested, Mister Bowman; why do you look like the bird that just escaped the snake every time we look at each other."

Ellis's blue gaze showed amusement when he answered. "I guess because, for a fact, I did escape the snake. Until you showed up with Jake and his unloaded gun, I'd just about run out of clever ideas to stay alive . . . The other reason don't have anything to do with gratitude because you saved my bacon. It's got to do with when we looked at each other last night—you passin' the jailhouse about dusk in a top-buggy, and me standin' on a stool looking out a window in the jailhouse. You remember that?"

Sam Hanks did not answer. Up where they had left Thompson and his friend there were puddling shadows. They were diluted and runty, but at least afternoon had arrived, the sun had slipped off-center, and the blindfolded men were talking very earnestly to each other.

Ellis ignored all those things and continued to gaze at the lithe, slightly shorter person walking beside him. "Sam? You remember that?"

"Yes. And you guessed when I came around from behind the tree this morning?"

"No. I guessed last night Sam Hanks was a woman. This morning when you showed up, I was plumb convinced of it. Sam, it must be hot inside that old coat."

"It is hot."

"Then take it off. They can't see you."

Sam Hanks looked up. "No. Maybe later. Do you see a faint patch up yonder at the northeast edge of this glade?"

Ellis looked and saw nothing. "No ma'm. What of it?"

"That's where we're going to take them. That's where I can take the hat and coat off."

"And keep them blindfolded?"

"It won't matter by then, Mister Bowman."

"Sam, Mister Bowman was my paw and I never knew him. I'm Ellis. Just plain Ellis . . . Why won't it matter then?"

But they were within hearing distance of the captives and

Sam Hanks did not reply. In fact her attitude changed from the easy way it had been out near the horses, back to what it had been otherwise all morning. She shoved Marshal Thompson and said, "Walk."

He balked. "Take the damned rag off my eyes."

Sam Hanks shoved a sixgun barrel into the large man's back and Thompson began walking, but hesitantly and awkwardly. Jake fared better. Ellis took him by the arm and walked with him, and when they halted for Ellis to explain that they had to jump a little swift-water creek hidden in rank grass, he used the interlude to remove Jake's shellbelt and holstered Colt, and buckle them into place around his own middle. After they were across the creek he methodically reloaded the gun from shellbelt loops.

Jake was unsteady through the rank grass. "How much farther?" he asked.

Ellis did not know, but they were nearing the upper curve of timber where Sam had said there was a trail. He did not think it would be much farther. "Just keep walking," he said.

"What's the sense of keepin' this rag over my eyes? I'm not goin' to say anythin' because I got no idea where I am."

"Shut up, Jake," Bowman said offhandedly. "I got no idea where we are either. I'm not the head Indian, Sam Hanks is. If Sam Hanks wants you blindfolded, then you're going to be blindfolded. Just walk, and don't worry, I'm not going to let you fall."

There was a trail and Sam herded Marshal Thompson up it. Thompson stopped trying to test each forward step, evidently satisfied that the trail underfoot was not going to lead him face-first into a big tree.

There was a second clearing, smaller this time, no more than ten or fifteen acres in size. In the middle of it was another log cabin, but this one had glass windows in the front wall and a stone chimney. To one side there was a corral of peeled poles with a ditch carrying diverted creek water passing through one corner of it.

Ellis wondered at the tidiness of the cabin and admired its scenic setting. He turned the horses into the corral, leaned briefly on the pole gate looking around, then went over to the cabin—and halted dead-still in the doorway.

Sam Hanks had shed the long old coat and the disreputable hat. Ellis had known a lot of people named Sam, but this was the first person by that name who had ever stopped his breath for three seconds.

The prisoners were seated at a hand-made rough wooden table, hunched forward on benches. At the far side of the table Sam Hanks reddened under Ellis Bowman's wide-eyed and admiring stare, then turned away to stoke up a small fire in a cast-iron stove and put a coffeepot atop it.

Ellis kicked one of those little benches around and dropped down on it, still watching the woman with the curly sorrel-blond hair over by the stove. His attention was diverted when Marshal Thompson growled. "How long you goin' to keep this up? My arms are numb."

Sam turned, ignored Ellis and returned to the table to stand at the head of it, her sixgun in hand. She nodded to Ellis to untie the hands of their prisoners. Nothing was said about the blindfolds so he left them in place and when Jake finished flexing both arms and would have reached upwards, Ellis rapped him on the chest. "Put your hands on the table." Jake obeyed. So did Marshal Thompson; being unable to see he had evidently thought that command meant him too.

Sam Hanks was still avoiding Ellis's gaze, but now it was obviously not to avoid being embarrassed by his wide-eyed admiring stare. "Marshal," said Sam. "Take off your blindfold."

Ellis watched. When the cloth had been pulled down where it hung draped like a neckerchief Marshal Thompson's eyes sprang wide open, his coarse features seemed frozen, and the big upper body which had been slumped, drew up erectly stiff. He said, "You!" in an explosive burst of breath. "I . . .

There was something . . . I had a feelin' I knew you back up on the meadow."

The green eyes were dead-level and unmoving, but Sam said nothing for a long time, not until Will Thompson had made a flapping gesture with his arms, then planted both elbows atop the table and leaned on them gazing steadily at Sam Hanks. "There was something about you . . . It would have come to me."

Sam swung her sixgun in his direction. "You were going to kill him, weren't you, Marshal?"

"Kill who?"

The green eyes flashed. "You know who—Bowman. You've had practice at back-shooting, among other things."

Thompson's face reddened and his massive, square jaw settled solidly. "Wait a minute. He said he saw the bank robber hide something back up there . . . My job is to find stolen money and keep order."

Sam Hanks's mouth drooped. "And steal. And kill. And—"

"You've got no proof," exclaimed the large lawman. "There never was no proof it didn't happen the way everyone believes it happened."

Sam's gaze was bitterly cold. "Marshal, everyone isn't up here. Just you and I are up here, and it's taken a long time for the opportunity to come along for me to get you up here." Sam raised an arm and pointed. "See that old branding iron?" All three men looked toward the stove where an iron with its base buried in the sand of the box under and around the stove was leaning. The rounded hand-holding upper segment of the iron was visible as was about twenty-four inches of its shank, but the bottom part where the brand itself was, did not show.

"That's about all that is left, Marshal."

Will Thompson was unimpressed and shrugged mighty shoulders. "Then you got a souvenir," he said, his rattlesnake eyes watching her gun hand.

Sam Hanks's green eyes darkened with irony. "A souvenir? That's not why I brought it up here, Marshal, nor why I've kept it over the years."

Ellis, trying to grasp bits and pieces of what this might be all about, saw the big lawman studying the handsome green-eyed woman. Clearly, the woman and the lawman had just faced something only they understood. Then Marshal Thompson gently wagged his head. "You . . . That happened about five years back. Everyone knows how it happened, and you can't make anything different out of it."

"Mr. Bowman," Sam said, "please guard the prisoners for a moment."

Ellis stood next to her, with Jake's reloaded sixgun in hand, while she filled three tin cups with black coffee and set them on the table. Then she picked up her sixgun and motioned Ellis to sit down.

She renewed the discussion where it had been interrupted by saying, "I can do it, Marshal. I've been practicing for a long while."

Thompson looked across at Ellis, his gaze contemptuous. He put the same look upon Jake Mitchell. But when he spoke again it was to the woman. "I don't think so, an' I don't think you're goin' to try it, because if you figured to do that when you brought us here, you wouldn't have untied our arms . . . Lady, I don't care whether you got one gun or ten, if you try using that iron I'm not goin' to just set here and let you do it."

The green eyes were unblinking and unwavering as the handsome woman lazily swung her sixgun to bear on Marshal Thompson, and looking him squarely in the eye, cocked it.

Thompson's scornful expression faded a little. He looked from her face to the weapon aimed at him, then back to her face, and then to Bowman, whose hand rested on his holstered sixgun.

Ellis Bowman would not have wagered a lead penny that she would not kill the large man. And at that distance, half the length and width of a table, one slug from her sixgun would make the inside of her cabin resemble a slaughter-house.

Ellis reached for his cup and half drained it, then put it down, hard. Jake jumped. Without the blindfold his face was gray. He had faced her sixgun before, but it had not been cocked the other time. He had felt sure when "Sam Hanks" had come up behind him, that "he" could kill a man. What caused a renewed flooding of sweat under Jake's shirt was that he was sitting on the same side of the table as Will Thompson, and only about three feet farther away. At that range if the lady fired, even if her slug tore Thompson apart, it would still have more than enough momentum left to hit him. Jake's nerves were crawling like snakes under his skin.

# CHAPTER 9
# Sam

FOR Ellis, there were several considerations, not the least of which was that he had no intention of sitting at a table watching a man get shot to death. For another, he was as hungry as a cub bear, and finally, he had been listening to something he did not understand for about as long as he wanted to. So he arose without a word, and with Sam's surprised green eyes following everything he did, Ellis went back around behind Thompson and Jake without a glance in her direction, growled for the prisoners to put both arms behind themselves, and despite some unpleasantness, lashed them tightly.

"Don't either of you leave this table," he said quietly.

Jake's face was white. Marshal Thompson glared, so Ellis poked his chest with a stiff finger, "Don't get up from the table. Don't even think about it."

Then Ellis turned to Sam. "We're going outside for a little talk. Put that gun in its holster."

Despite the passing afternoon it was hot in the cabin. Silently she crossed to the west wall and raised the window to allow the air to circulate. Then she walked to the door with Ellis, looked over her shoulder once, and preceded him outside.

There was shade on the east side of the cabin so he took her around there where the wall was solid and would hinder eavesdropping by the men inside. He leaned against the adzed logs gazing at her. Without that old coat she was all woman and with her face slightly tilted and shiny, he thought her as pretty as a speckled bird. He hooked both thumbs in

Jake's shellbelt and said nothing for a moment. Then he asked: "What is your name?"

"Samantha Coe."

"Why are you so dead-set on killing the marshal?"

"It is a very long story. We'd need the rest of the day for me to explain it to you."

Ellis shifted position on the log wall, looked over across the pretty little glade where somber dark green cut off the view beyond the first few ranks of big sugar pines. "We're not goin' anywhere," he told her. "I got plenty of time—all the rest of the year in fact . . . You want to tell me what this is all about?"

"We can't leave them in there like that. You don't know Will Thompson."

"Lady, you might be surprised how well I know Marshal Thompson." He told her about being captured at the other cabin, about his money the marshal had taken from him, and he also told her what he felt certain had been in store for him when they had ridden up to Custer Meadow before daylight. The more he said, the more sardonic her face became, and when he had finished she gazed at him the way a mother would look at a child.

"You've figured him out exactly right. I knew what he and Jake had in mind, which was why I rode up here last night and waited for them. If I'd known about your twelve thousand dollars I'd have gone after him instead of Mitchell—who's a hard-drinking rangeman who hangs around town picking up odd jobs when he can."

Ellis waited until she had finished. "All right, Sam. I told you my troubles, now how about you tellin' me your troubles? Start off with this business of using the name of some old gaffer who's been dead for five or six years. Sam Hanks."

There was an interruption; a faintly-heard rustle of sound from within the cabin. Ellis shoved off the wall, put his ear to it for a moment, then turned with a finger over his lips and moved soundlessly away. She watched him but remained where she was, even when he had disappeared around the corner of the cabin to slip soundlessly along the back wall.

At the west corner he stopped, waited, then eased his head around. The sounds had ceased, there was no one in sight: he dropped into a low crouch, palmed Jake's reloaded sixgun and crept ahead bent nearly double until he was below the window Samantha Coe had opened.

Inch by inch he raised up, bringing the gun up with him. When his forehead and eyes were even with the sill he could see them, one on each side of the doorway. Jake had a twelve-inch scantling from the woodbox in his fist. He was on the east side of the door. Marshal Thompson was on the opposite side holding that old branding iron in his right fist, poised to strike the moment someone came through the doorway.

Ellis raised up very slowly, pushed the gun through and cocked it. Jake's head snapped around, eyes bulging. Thompson came half around, his face twisted into an expression of defiance.

Ellis leaned on the sill looking in at them. He nodded to Jake. "Drop it." Jake let the piece of wood fall. Ellis looked at the large lawman. "You too—drop it!"

As he had done before when he had been cornered, Marshal Thompson hesitated, his muscles bunching to throw the iron at Ellis.

"Drop it or I'll drop you, Marshal!"

The big man opened his fist. The branding iron fell to the plank floor, but the fury was still in his glare as Ellis stood looking at them. "How did you get those bindings off?" he asked Jake, knowing he would not get anything but a snarl from Thompson.

Jake was white in the face again. "I used my teeth to get the rope off'n him, then he got me free."

Ellis raised his voice. "Sam! Go around where you can see the front door. They're coming out. If either one of them tries to rush you or run, shoot him. Samantha, you hear me?"

She answered curtly. "All right."

Ellis wagged Jake's sixgun. "Marshal, you get clever again and you won't have to wait for her to do it. I'll do it for her. Walk outside!"

He waited until he heard Samantha order them to stop walking, then he crept down the log wall and into the slanting sunrays out front. He told her what they had done and what they were waiting to do, put up his weapon and eyed the pair of men looking back at him. He felt no particular anger toward either Jake or the lawman, just exasperation.

"All right. You two walk out into the meadow. Go east until I tell you to stop. Then you stand out there until I tell you to do something else."

They obeyed. With a distance of roughly a hundred feet between the prisoners and the cabin, Ellis told them to stop walking and lie down on their backs. When they did exactly as he had said, Ellis motioned for Samantha to put up her weapon and led the way to the east wall where the shade was deepening, and shoved back his hat while eyeing the captives.

She said, "I told you about him."

Ellis nodded. "Yep. Well, let's see how he makes out this time. Maybe he can make himself invisible, or sprout wings and fly straight up out of gun-range." He smiled at her but she did not notice because she was walking back around toward the front of the cabin. He watched but said nothing. When she returned she was holding the old branding iron. He took it from her and examined it. The iron had been forged by someone who believed in using plenty of steel. Whoever he had been, he had been good at hammering and shaping, good even at fluxing welds over an anvil while they were still red from a forge, but the thing was poorly balanced and very heavy. At the end of a marking day a man who had used this old iron for about eight or ten hours would expect his right arm to fall off.

Samantha raised the branding end. It was a horseshoe. At least it had been formed to resemble one, but it was thicker, wider between the heels and heavier than most horseshoes. Still, it was a good resemblance, a marking iron that seared a horseshoe brand on cattle.

She watched him lean the iron aside and raise his eyes to the men, who had not moved, and who were watching Ellis and the woman without even speaking to one another.

She glanced out there now and then, but once she started speaking, it was clear to Ellis Bowman that the only thing in her mind was what she had to say.

"That was Sam Hanks's marking iron. He made it. There were three of them. One is missing and was never found. I have the other two—this one, and its mate at my house down at Batesville." She paused, staring at the leaning iron. When she spoke again her voice was different, slower and quieter, as though she were dredging up memories that were painful to put into words. During this time she did not look up at Ellis. She seemed particularly eager to avoid that.

"Sam Hanks' wife died. They had a baby and it died too. I was much younger when he used to ride down and visit my parents. He would always bring me something. One time it was a baby raccoon. I had it for years. Another time . . ." She stopped, shot him a look, reddened slightly and said, "I'm sorry . . . When I was about twelve he gave me a spotted horse. I used to ride up to the meadow and visit him. We'd work cattle or sometimes just go riding up through the mountains. My parents would come up sometimes too. My mother would scold Sam for not washing his clothes often enough or cleaning up his cabin. If he knew she'd be coming, he would work like a beaver to get the cabin spic and span . . . Ellis, I'm wandering again."

He smiled at her. "He was fond of you an' it sounds like you liked him."

"I loved him. He was so kind, and sometimes so quietly sad. My mother told my father Sam Hanks saw in me the child he had lost."

"Your folks didn't mind?"

CUSTER MEADOW ■ 71

"No, not at all. They were fond of Sam, too. He was part of the family. At Christmastime . . ."

Ellis cleared his throat. She shot him a look, and said she was sorry for digressing again, and started over. "He would hire men to trail out cattle in the autumn, and sometimes he would keep a couple of riders through the summer, but mostly he worked the ranch by himself—and I helped when I could. He taught me to shoot, even to shoe horses."

"Where was his ranch?" Ellis asked, with a very strong notion of the answer he was going to get.

"Custer Meadow. He owned all of it and even part of the mountains behind it."

"How many cattle did he run?"

"I don't think he knew. I made a few gate-cuts for him in the fall of the year, but we hadn't found all the cattle. My highest tally was nine hundred cows and six hundred steers. We didn't bring in the bulls . . . He guessed one time that he probably had about fifteen hundred head, all told, and I thought at the time there were many more."

Ellis watched Marshal Thompson fidgeting out in the meadow. "What happened to him, Sam?"

She also turned to look out where the lawman was squirming on the grass, her eyes darker green and nearly closed. "He could tell you." She faced back around. "Some pot hunters who used to go after game in the mountains each autumn found him dead in the corrals. He had been kicked to death. There was the clear imprint of a horseshoe in his face and on his forehead . . . Ellis?"

"Yes."

"I'd better wait to tell you the rest of it. Anyway, they brought him down to Batesville and buried him in the town cemetery, and that was when I cried hardest because Sam never would have wanted that. He would have wanted to be buried up on the meadow with his wife and baby."

"Whose idea was it to bury him at Batesville?"

"Marshall Thompson and Charles Turner who runs the

bank down there. He was brought to town one day and buried wrapped in a blanket the next day. They said because it was summertime it would be best to get him buried right away."

"Did you see him, Sam?"

"Yes. I went over to the embalming shed behind Mister Cuthbert's apothecary shop. It was awful."

"Sam?"

"Yes."

"What were you going to tell me a few minutes ago?"

She answered by picking up the horseshoe branding iron and holding it up for him to see. Without a word she leaned with the iron pressing against the log wall. She said, "What would that look like if the iron made a burn?"

He turned. "Like a horseshoe."

She scowled at him. "Ellis—how would this look?" She reversed the iron. He answered the same way, practically and quietly. "Like an upside-down horseshoe."

She continued to lean on the upside-down iron. "If a horse kicked a man to death, could he do it to leave an upside-down mark like that?"

Ellis said, "No, not unless he was lying on his back, an' horses can't kick. . . ." He let it trail off because she was looking exultantly at him. He looked at the upside-down iron again before slowly bringing his gaze back to her face. "Not like that, Sam."

"Exactly like that. The toe cleat made a terrible wound in his forehead." She leaned the iron back against the house and turned to squint out where the lawman and his companion were standing. "I've been horse-kicked. You probably have too."

He nodded ruefully. "Dozens of times."

"Ellis, when a horse kicks with his hind hooves, the calks are up—they point toward the sky. Like you said, for a horse to kick a man with the calks pointing downward he would have to be upside-down, on his back."

Ellis plucked a drying stem of grass and chewed on it as he studied the two men lying a revolver-shot away in the grass. He spat out the stalk and asked, "Are you plumb sure that is what you saw on the old man's body?"

"Absolutely certain."

"Who else noticed it?"

"I don't think anyone did, or, if they did, they did not say anything about it. Marshal Thompson said Sam Hanks had died of being kicked in the head while in a corral with some horses. That is the way the story is believed right now, years later, in town."

"How about your parents?"

"My father had the abstract office in Batesville. He knew next to nothing about horses and my mother knew even less, and one time when I told them what I thought, they looked at me like I'd lost my mind—so—I did not mention it again, to anyone."

"But you've had it festering in your heart all these years," he said, watching her face.

She looked at him, soft-eyed and pleading. "I loved him. He was wonderful to me, to everyone. He—"

"Sam, what happened to the cattle?"

She sagged a little. "I don't know, but a few weeks later when I rode up there by myself to cry a little for him, there were no cattle. And no horses. There were not even any fresh droppings in the grass."

"But why are you stirring things up now, after so many years?"

She lowered her face and said in a trembling voice, "My mother died a few years ago and I was busy making a life for my father and me. When he died last fall, I felt alone, helpless. There was nothing I could do about my parents' deaths, but at least I could try to avenge the murder of Sam Hanks."

Ellis did not ask what robbing a bank had to do with it, instead he raised a gentle hand to lift a coil of sorrel-blond hair from her forehead, and said, "I don't blame you. Let's fetch those two inside and make some supper. I'm starving."

# CHAPTER 10
# Riding in the Dark

JAKE was completely subdued. He and Marshal Thompson had undoubtedly discussed their situation while they were out on the grass, and when they were brought back to the cabin and seated at the table, Jake's eyes were rarely still. He would watch Samantha at the stove preparing a meal, then he would looked quickly at Ellis Bowman, whose hand was never far from his holster.

His companion, the big lawman from Batesville, sat hunched with both hands clasped on the tabletop considering Bowman. He was still defiant, but an hour or so out yonder lying on the meadow had provided him with plenty of time to consider his situation. Like it or not, a lot of things had gone wrong, and the man watching him from across the room was considerably more capable than Thompson had thought he would be. No matter what Thompson came up with, Bowman was one step ahead of him.

He might eventually have an opportunity to attack Bowman, but while he waited for that moment, he had considered several alternatives to just sitting and waiting.

He had been ignoring Samantha since coming back to the cabin. Not because he felt especially hostile toward her, but simply because he felt that Bowman was the person he would have to deal with.

He turned, watched Sam working at the stove, turned back and said, "Think about it, cowboy; whatever she told you is just goin' to get you in deeper, an' sooner or later most likely you'll get killed." Marshal Thompson gently wagged his head. "It ain't worth it. If I was in your boots I'd get on the ridgling and make tracks."

Ellis eyed the large man dispassionately. "No you wouldn't. And I won't do it either. You'd end up with my money."

Thompson leaned back as he made an expansive gesture and smiled. "You want your money back? Take me down to town an' I'll give it to you—and a twenty-four-hour head start."

Ellis matched the lawman's craggy smile. "I don't think so. Thompson, you're as treacherous as a scorpion. But I'll tell you what I will do—give us all the details about old Hanks's death, including what happened to his livestock, and when we get down to Batesville with you and Jake, I'll see to it you get a nice, rainproof cell in the Batesville jailhouse."

Marshal Thompson snorted his derision. Without even bothering to reply, he turned and watched Samantha preparing their supper. Then he said something that Ellis Bowman was satisfied had not surfaced impulsively.

"If you trust her, you'll be making a big mistake. But she's nice to look at, for a fact. A man notices that right off, don't he?"

Ellis began to have an inkling about Thompson's urges, but right now, with darkness covering the land he had something else on his mind, so when he spoke again to the lawman it was about something altogether different.

"How old are you?"

The question made Thompson blink. "Fifty. What the hell has that got to—"

"In fifty years, Marshal, somewhere down your backtrail I figure there's got to be some interesting facts a man could uncover about you."

Thompson sat in long silence looking at Ellis Bowman. He seemed uneasy but when Samantha brought their food all he said was, "Nobody's a saint, cowboy." Then he and Jake started eating. They were hungry. So was Ellis, though Samantha did not appear to have much of an appetite, and preferred to hold a sixgun on Thompson while Ellis ate.

Later, after Ellis had roughed-out a plan, he told Saman-

tha he was going to ride down to Batesville. He did not tell
her why because he preferred to let Thompson and Mitchell
worry.

She looked surprised but did not question him. He lashed
the arms of their prisoners in back again, pushed them to
the floor and bound their ankles as well, then nodded for
her to precede him outside. He stood a moment breathing
deeply of the scented darkness, then said, "Don't take your
eyes off them. Not for one minute. Especially Thompson. I'll
be back after sunup."

She nodded a trifle woodenly and still said nothing, so he
took her by the hand, led her beyond earshot of the cabin
and said, "I want to talk to the banker and a few other folks.
Sam, if you're right; if old Hanks was murdered, maybe that
could be concealed, but no one steals fifteen hundred head
of cattle without leaving signs of it all over the place."

She brushed his arm with her hand. "You'll have to be very
careful. Marshal Thompson may not be very well liked in
town, but he has friends."

Ellis nodded. He remembered the other possemen besides
Jake. "I'll be careful. You be even more careful."

He offered his hand. She took it, clung to it briefly, then
showed a brave smile. "I'll be watching for you."

He went around back to saddle the ridgling and when he
rode past the cabin she was still out front. She waved, he
waved back, then headed down toward the lower country
beyond that screen of big sugar pines they had passed
through to reach her secret glade with its cabin.

The night was softly lit by a rusty moon in one of its earlier
quarters, and an even more distant high rash of stars. He did
not know the best route to Batesville but he knew which
direction it would be in and that was the route he chose,
passing through a lot of broken country until he was riding
through low, gentle foothills.

He studied the position of the moon, made an estimate of

the distance he had to cover, and decided he would probably arrive in Batesville shortly before daylight.

As he rode, he thought about Samantha alone with two men who would probably murder her in an instant if the opportunity arose. And also about the things she had told him.

There was enough to keep him occupied for the full distance he had to cover. By the time he felt the chill of predawn, he knew Batesville had to be close. He had worked out a rough idea of what he would say to the people he wanted to talk to.

There was something else he wanted to do, but unless he could enter Batesville in the dark he probably would be unable to do it. A man could not just walk into the jailhouse in broad daylight and ransack the place.

But because he finally got down there and it was still dark, although a hint of gray showed along the farthest eastward horizon, he decided to try the jailhouse. He left his horse out back and entered the building through the storeroom, plunging into inky darkness.

The moon was gone, the cold was capable of stiffening a man's joints, but inside the jailhouse it was almost warm.

He had entered by a simple expedient. He had picked up a small crowbar leaning against the alley fence, and had inserted it inside the padlock's loop, then leaned his weight downward gently and with all his strength. The padlock had withstood most of his weight but not all of it. The mechanism was ruined when the lock was forced open. He left it hanging in the hasp.

He lit the office lamp, shielded it from the roadway windows with his hat, and went to work sifting through everything he could find in desk drawers and wooden boxes against the wall behind the desk. Those boxes contained nothing but wanted dodgers, some of which were fairly recent, some of which went back almost eight years.

He did not have enough time to make a study of the

dodgers, and they might not have told him much if he'd had the time, so he went back to the desk. Several dogs barked and someone wearing heavy boots strode past in a southerly direction, making Ellis cover the lantern until the footfalls sounded farther away.

He gave up his search and returned to the alley, taking the broken brass padlock with him. He waited until he had led his horse down almost to the rear entrance of the liverybarn before hiding the broken padlock. Then he walked into the barn's runway where a man, who had evidently just arrived to get ready for the day's business, was standing outside a harness-room, waiting for the coffee to get hot on the harness-room stove. He watched Bowman approach in dingy gloom, and showed a tentative smile as he said, "Good morning. I get a lot of folks heading out this time of day but not too many heading in."

As Ellis handed over the reins he said, "Stall him with hay and grain. If you turn him into a corral you'll regret it. He's a ridgling."

The liveryman's curiosity about his first customer of the day vanished before what he had just been told about the muscled-up thousand-pound bay horse. In his business ridglings were anathema. He looked the horse over, then asked if he bit. Ellis had never been bitten by the horse so he said, "Not as far as I know. But that's sure something they're known for . . . He's well-mannered and quiet. Still an' all, unless you want your mares brought to heat and your geldings chewed up, keep him in a stall."

The liveryman was nodding his head and eyeing the bay horse. He had lost all interest in the ridgling's owner until Ellis asked what time the cafe opened.

"About a half hour from now. Actually, he's in there right now gettin' ready for the breakfast trade, but he won't unlock the door for another half hour . . . Pretty hungry are you?"

Ellis nodded. "I could eat . . . Is the marshal around?"

The liveryman was holding a pair of rawhide reins and

looking at the docile ridgling when he answered. "Not that I know of. I heard at the saloon last night he ain't been in town since maybe night before last."

Ellis strolled up through to the front roadway. There was, indeed, light behind the cafe's fogged-up front window. There were several other lights along Main Street as well, which was encouraging. The light he gazed at longest came through a narrow roadway window. Unlike most of the other lights, this one had a faint but noticeable blue tint to it. It also shone in a reflected way off a signboard jutting outward above the front doorway.

That little narrow building sandwiched between larger, bolder-looking business establishments was the apothecary's shop. That was what the sign said, anyway.

Ellis saw a moving, rather vague shadow, pass behind a counter and moments later the bluish lamp was blown out. There was a second lamp farther back, visible through an open door. A narrow-shouldered silhouette passed from the front of the store into the room where the second light was glowing.

Ellis crossed the empty roadway and rapped lightly on the apothecary's door. He had to rap three times before a man shuffled from the back room and peered out first, then unlocked the door and moved aside for Bowman to enter. As the older man was closing the door he ran a quick look up and down his visitor, then said, "The shop isn't really open for trade just yet, but if you'll come back to my mixing room . . ." The old man offered an almost apologetic smile and led the way.

The room where the bright lamp was glowing had shelves on all four walls, a small desk and a much larger working area where pestles and mortars, an assortment of odd-shaped small spoons hung neatly against the wall above a large, thick slab of marble.

As the apothecary turned for a better look at his visitor, Ellis saw his eyes widen. Until this moment Ellis had not thought about his appearance. He needed a shave, his clothing was rumpled and soiled, and he towered over the smaller, older and much more frail man. He smiled as he told the old man his name. This seemed to alleviate some of the apothecary's uneasiness, but Ellis's next words brought back the uneasy look.

"A few years back they tell me you helped bury a man named Sam Hanks."

The apothecary bobbed his head like a bird and moved closer to his desk. "Yes. Close to six years ago it was. I do undertaking along with my regular business. Sometimes I do doctoring as well . . . Were you a friend of old Sam Hanks?"

Ellis ignored the question to ask one of his own. "Do you recollect what caused his death?"

The apothecary jumped his eyes away then back and felt behind him for his desk chair. He sat down looking up at the larger and younger man. "Yes, I recollect that, Mister Bowman. What I'd like to know is what your interest is."

Ellis stepped toward the desk and the old man cringed away. Ellis picked up a pencil, turned a scrap of paper and drew two horseshoes, one with the calks facing downward, one with them facing upward. Then he tossed down the pencil and smiled at the old man. "Which way were the calks of the horseshoe that killed Mister Hanks pointing?"

The reaction to his question and the drawings would have been noticeable in poorer light. The old man swallowed hard, ran an unsteady hand up his vest to a heavy gold watch chain, and twisted it between his fingers while staring at the drawings. His color, which was not ruddy, seemed to Ellis to pale toward gray, and when the apothecary fished in a metal case for a pair of rimless spectacles, which he unsteadily hooked into place, his face had slackened. After a long study of the drawings, he turned his head without turning the rest of his body. "That was a long time ago," he said in a faint voice.

Ellis nodded. "Five years. But a man would remember something that unusual wouldn't he?"

The apothecary's pale eyes sank to the holstered Colt on his visitor's hip, then returned to the drawings. "Yes, a man would remember, Mister Bowman," he murmured, and continued to gaze at the drawings for a long while without speaking again.

There was daylight beyond the window and a slight stir of activity along the roadway. Ellis leaned down to study the drawings, and his proximity to the frail old man in the chair brought a faint and grudging statement from the apothecary.

"Up, Mister Bowman. The calks pointed upwards, the full force of the shoe struck Mister Hanks between the mouth and the forehead . . . but the calks were thick and raised. They tore his face something awful."

Ellis looked at the older man, who seemed mesmerized by the drawings and did not raise his head. Ellis stepped back. "I don't expect a man in your trade would know a hell of a lot about horses and their shoes and how they kick, would he?"

The older man eased back gingerly in his chair, removed the glasses and began to gently polish them with a white handkerchief. As he did this he said, "No, a man in my trade wouldn't, but then I haven't always been in this line of work . . . Thirty-five years ago I was in the federal cavalry. That was back during the war. Most likely you was very young back then." The old man carefully folded his glasses and put them back in their metal case. When he had finished doing this, he looked straight at Ellis Bowman. "I'd like for you to explain something to me, Mister Bowman: Are you by any chance a friend of our town marshal, Mister Thompson?"

Ellis shook his head as he returned the old man's gaze.

The apothecary seemed to accept that, but if it mitigated his nervousness, Ellis saw no sign of it. Then the old man said, "Do you expect we are thinking the same thing, Mister Bowman?"

Ellis nodded his head. "We might be . . . A horse would

have to be upside-down for the toe cleat to punch a hole in his forehead. I've never heard of a horse being able to kick while he was lying on his back, but even if one did, seems to me it would be impossible for him to kick that hard while he was upside-down."

The apothecary put his glasses case on the drawing and rolled the gold watch-chain between his fingers again, looking toward the open door where daylight was beginning to brighten his gloomy little store.

"It's possible," he finally said. "But the horse would have to have his shoes nailed on upside down, wouldn't he, and that's not likely to be done is it, Mister Bowman?"

Ellis smiled at the old man, whose color was returning and whose nervousness appeared to have abated a little. "There wouldn't be any point in nailing shoes on a horse that way, but what I'm interested in is—who besides you noticed that the horseshoe imprint that killed Mister Hanks was upside-down?"

"I don't think anyone else noticed it because only a few people saw Mister Hanks before they buried him in his blanket. There was a little girl—she's a grown woman now—and her folks, but otherwise as near as I can recall, there was only me and Marshal Thompson."

Ellis offered his hand. After a moment of regarding it the old man shook it and arose from his chair. "This is something it don't do any good to talk about, Mister Bowman. I'd expect you not to mention me if it ever comes up. I'd surely appreciate it if you didn't."

# CHAPTER 11
# A Couple of Surprises

THE tonsorial parlor was open for business. The barber was a fat man with a complexion women would have envied him for. He was either an unusual barber or else he was one of those people who did not get talkative early in the morning, but in either case while he was shearing Bowman and shaving him, the only thing he commented on was the weather.

Ellis nearly went to sleep in the barber chair. He had reason; it had been more than twenty-four hours since he'd been able to sleep, and even then he had not slept very well.

Finally, too, the cafe was open. Ellis had a little difficulty finding a place along the counter. Quite a number of men who were either unmarried or who went to work before their wives were out of bed, were eating and gossiping while the tall, cadaverous-looking man who owned the cafe hurried back and forth filling cups and delivering platters. He barely glanced at Bowman. It was ten minutes before he brought a platter of hard-fried eggs with slices of steak cooked into them, a mound of potatoes, some toast, and went back for the slice of blueberry pie that completed the meal. The cafeman had been serving this same breakfast for three months. Even at suppertime when there was no rush, he did not offer much in the way of a selection, and unless townsmen knew where else to eat in a town that had only one cafe, they took what was placed in front of them.

Ellis did not look up once he began eating. He had not been conscious of his hunger until he had forked in the first mouthful. Men came and went but two diners who had been watching Ellis since he had entered, remained at the counter toying with coffee cups. When Ellis finally pushed the platter away and arose to count out some silver coins, the pair of staring townsmen drifted out front, walked northward a few doors and halted to watch.

As Ellis struck out on a diagonal course in the direction of the brick bank building, the two townsmen waited until he had entered the building, then hurried in the direction of the emporium.

The sun was rising and most of the morning chill was being burned off when a slight man wearing a handsome brocaded vest with black sleeve-protectors and a green eye-shade came to his wicket and peered impassively out at Ellis. There was no welcome in his sallow face, but the hazel eyes behind his steel-rimmed glasses were inquisitively direct as he said, "Can I help you?"

Ellis jutted his jaw in the direction of a large, fleshy man smoking a cigar and sitting at a desk with his coat draped over the back of his chair. "Is that Mister Turner?" he asked, and the poker-faced clerk, whose chin receded into his neck, nodded his head. "I'd like to talk to him," Ellis said. The clerk dutifully slid off his stool and approached the desk set at an angle near the rear of the room so that the fleshy man would be able to see in all directions.

Ellis saw the clerk speak, saw the fleshy man remove his cigar and glance toward the wicket, and bob his head, impatiently Ellis thought. The clerk returned to hold aside a little panel and point toward the large man. "He's very busy this morning," he said.

Ellis did not smile when Charley Turner arose and offered his hand. But he pumped the soft paw, dropped it, and waited for the banker to resume his seat. When Turner waved toward an empty chair, Ellis continued to stand, thumbs hooked in his shellbelt, gazing downward. As the banker's brow creased Ellis said, "I'm the feller Marshal Thompson had in jail."

Charley Turner's expression underwent a swift change and the hand hovering above the cigar in its big glass ashtray did not move until Turner had looked up more slowly, making his banker's assessment of the stranger in front of his desk. Then he picked up the cigar and smiled. "I thought you'd be a hundred miles off by now . . . What was the name?"

"Bowman. Ellis Bowman. No, I didn't head out . . . There is about twelve thousand dollars of my money in the marshal's safe, Mister Turner. I was told you said it was stolen from this bank."

Charley Turner forgot to keep up a head of smoke and his stogie died. "Who told you that? That is exactly what I told Will Thompson was not the case . . . Well, at first I thought it was, then my clerk told me the eleven thousand robbed from the bank was brand new money, no stains or creases or wrinkles on any of it. Boxed at the Denver mint and delivered down here still in the box." Charley Turner studied the freshly-shaved man in front of his desk. "Who told you I said your money belonged to the bank, Mister Bowman?"

Ellis continued to stand hipshot, thumbs hooked, looking down at the banker. "A local gent, who said he had a fortune in your bank."

Turner put the cigar aside again. He leaned back looking up at Bowman. "No one has a fortune in our bank, Mister Bowman. Sometimes the stockmen sell off a big gather and bring the money to us for safekeeping, but they usually take it out again. Stockmen aren't very trusting souls."

Ellis said, "Marshal Thompson told me—he's the one with the fortune in your bank."

Charley Turner sat very still looking up, then he lowered his head and shook it. "Mister Bowman, I just told you, no one has a fortune in this bank. As for Will Thompson . . ."

"Yes? What about him?"

Turner glanced past at the wicket where his clerk was taking a deposit and doing the necessary paperwork. He did not seem likely to continue the conversation so Ellis primed him with a question. "What interested me, Mister Turner, was how anyone could have a big account with your bank on a town marshal's wages?"

"I told you, Mister Bowman, Marshal Thompson does not have an account with us."

Ellis shifted his stance slightly and continued to stare at the fleshy seated man. "Someone is a liar, Mister Turner. You or Will Thompson. I hope it's you because Will told me he knows where eleven thousand dollars is cached, and we're goin' to share it just as soon as I get back up in the mountains where he's guardin' the cache."

There was not one word of truth in Ellis's statement. He had gambled on upsetting the banker so badly that Turner would not wonder about some inconsistencies, one of which was that no man would ride off leaving another man alone with eleven thousand dollars, and really believe he or the money would still be there when his associate got back.

Turner arose slowly from the desk staring at Bowman. "Why would Will do a thing like that, when he already has your twelve thousand dollars in his safe? I know it was there because I counted it myself."

"Greed," stated Bowman.

The banker exploded, his neck swelled and his face reddened. When he spoke the clerk at his wicket flinched and hunched his shoulders and would not have turned around if his life had depended upon it.

"Greed? Greed for Chris' sake! That's the bank's money and he knows it. Has he gone crazy? He can't get away with this and neither can you! I'll have federal marshals in here!"

Almost as abruptly as the explosion had erupted it ended, but Charley Turner's face was still red and contorted. Only his glaring eyes narrowed. He remained stiffly erect for another moment, then sat down again, glaring from slitted eyes at something beyond Ellis Bowman. He picked up the dead cigar with a shaking hand, clamped it between his teeth and brought his icy gaze back to the husky man who had stood silently relaxed as the storm had broken over him.

Turner ground on the cigar and spoke so softly Ellis had to concentrate to hear him.

"All right. I don't know what's going on with you and Will Thompson—except that you're both crooks—but all right; now you take a message back to Will for me." Turner paused as though fitting words together. "You tell Will that I'm going to empty his account and hold it in the vault until he rides in here and hands me that eleven thousand dollars. Do you understand that?"

Ellis nodded, still standing hipshot with both thumbs hooked in his shellbelt. "I'll tell him . . . Mister Turner, you told me he didn't have an account."

The banker's rage had been so overpowering he had to sit a moment staring at the younger man before he even remembered having said that. He sputtered, flung the cigar into a brass cuspidor beside the desk, and finally said, "Well . . . He does have an account, but the bank's business is confidential."

"How big an account, Mister Turner?"

The banker's eyes wavered, then got steady and irate again. "That's none of your business."

Ellis methodically moved his right hand, drew Jake's gun with deliberation, pointed it at Charley Turner and said, "One more time, Mister Turner: How big an account?"

He cocked the gun.

Finally, the clerk had to turn, but that was all he did. His eyes were bulging. He stared at the cocked sixgun in Bowman's steady fist with almost the identical expression of pure terror that was mottling Charley Turner's fleshy features.

Ellis leaned and shoved the cocked gun closer. "I told you; that was the last time I'd ask you."

The banker raised a thick hand to his shirt-front and balled the cloth in a fist. He was having difficulty breathing but managed to whisper. "Thirty-eight thousand dollars."

Ellis let his breath out slowly, then spoke. "A man drawing

wages as a town marshal would have to be a real saving individual to cache away that kind of money, wouldn't he?"

Turner was really having trouble getting air. He sank back in the chair. His clerk jumped down from his stool and ran forward. As he passed Ellis, who was holstering his gun, the clerk said, "Do you know what you did? He's got a bad heart . . . Oh Jesus, I got to get Jed Cuthbert."

As the clerk fled from the building, Ellis walked easily to the front roadway. Outside the building, everything looked normal. There were women in bonnets carrying mesh bags in the direction of the general store, several stage passengers in the attire of city people were enjoying the shade out front of Wheeler's Waterhole Saloon, and farther down, in the direction of the liverybarn which Ellis turned toward without haste, there were three men leaning in tree shade seemingly carrying on a desultory conversation.

He did not cross over until he was near the blacksmith's shop, several hundred feet below those three slouching men, and they seemed to pay no attention to his progress. One had been whittling. He did not close and pocket his clasp-knife until Ellis strolled from sight down the liverybarn runway. Then the whittler, a lanky, stooped, nondescript individual with teeth stained brown from tobacco, jerked his head. His companions followed him almost to the cotton-wood shade in front of the barn, then one of them turned down alongside the building heading for the alleyway where he could cover anyone leaving the barn from that direction.

The lanky man paused, glanced at his companion and smiled. "Either he's got it around his belly again under his shirt, or Will went an' locked it in his safe. Either way we're goin' to get it . . . You ready, Everett?"

The other man loosened his gun in its hip-holster and solemnly nodded his head.

# CHAPTER 12
# The Possemen

THE liveryman emerged from his harness-room sucking his teeth. He'd had breakfast up at the cafe, had noticed Bowman up there, and gazed a little pensively at him as Ellis flipped the man half a cartwheel and asked for his horse.

The liveryman pocketed the silver half-dollar, which was more than he would have charged if he'd kept the horse one full day, and dutifully took down a shank and headed for a stall on the south side of the dingy runway two-thirds of the way toward the alley. He talked as he walked. "You was dead right—he's cranky all right. I just led a mare past his stall an' he commenced faunching and rollin' up his lip." The man halted at the door gazing in at the big bay ridgling. He did not seem anxious to go inside for the horse. "Good built animal, though, ain't he? And tough. If there's one thing I know about them, it's that they're tougher'n a boiled owl."

Ellis took the shank and opened the stall door. "Smart too," he said.

The liveryman watched the horse put his head down to be caught. "Yeah, that's what I've always heard; they're smarter'n other horses. I've owned a few but never by choice. I'd get 'em in trades. . . . The hell of it is a man don't know he's got one. They look just like a gelding from up on top or from down underneath. But when a man turns one into a corralful of other horses he damned soon finds out, what with the squealing and fighting and whatnot."

As Ellis led his horse forth the liveryman stepped aside eyeing the muscular animal. "The minute I know I got one, I get rid of him. Sometimes I even have to lose money, but anything is better'n having all your livestock chewed up, ain't it?"

Ellis led his horse to the post in front of the harness-room and carelessly looped the shank. He was moving toward the doorway when two men appeared out in the sunbright front roadway heading for the runway. He glanced around, then halted in the doorway and looked more closely. They looked familiar. He ducked back into the smelly little dingy room when he remembered where he had seen them. They were two of the possemen Marshal Thompson had brought up to the old cabin on Custer Meadow the morning he had disarmed and arrested Ellis.

There are times when instinct becomes very strong. This was one of those times. The morning he had been caught at the Hanks cabin neither Marshal Thompson nor his possemen had impressed Ellis as paragons of virtue, and now, knowing as much as he did about both Jake and the marshal, his instinct was shrilling a warning.

The liveryman came over to the harness-room door. He had not noticed the newcomers up front. As he stepped into the opening, he stopped dead still. Ellis was facing the door making no move toward his saddle, bridle and blanket on a rack. The liveryman's confusion lasted only until Ellis said, "You got a couple of visitors up front."

The liveryman rocked back and turned his head. The pair of possemen were approaching through the perpetual gloom of the long runway. He considered them briefly. "That's just Everett Jonas and Arnie Slocum."

Ellis looked steadily at the liverymen. "Do they board horses here?"

The older man shook his head. "Naw. They live in a shack at the north end of town, got a corral up there." The liveryman, too, seemed to be puzzled. He would have backed out the doorway if Ellis hadn't drawn his sixgun and leveled it at him. "Take them toward the rear alley. Say anythin' you got to say to get them to follow you. Move!"

The liveryman lost his color and turned worriedly to regard the pair of possemen, who were approaching with sunshine at their backs. He pulled himself together and with a horsetrader's professional affability, greeted them. " 'Morning, Arnie. 'Morning Ev. You boys care to look at a wild horse I took in last night? He's somethin' to see. Got him down here near—"

The possemen halted, stared at the liveryman, at the ridgling standing nearby, then one of them looked around as he said, "A feller come in here a few minutes go. Where'd he go?"

The liveryman cocked a thumb. "Across the alley I think. I was havin' coffee and didn't pay much attention. . . . Why, you boys know him?"

The man who had spoken was tall, thin, and had badly stained teeth. "Yeah, we know him," he replied, and looked toward the alley where sunlight showed brilliantly. The man he had sent around there should be in place. But maybe the feller from Custer Meadow had got out there before. The townsmen seemed to have difficulty arriving at a solution, but eventually he said, "Ev, go take a look. See if he's out there."

As Ev walked in the direction of the back alley, the tall, thin man relaxed, looking more annoyed than worried. He addressed the liveryman again. "That's the feller who robbed the bank. Will had him locked up."

Ellis saw the liveryman's back stiffen. He could not see his face. After an interval of silence the liveryman noisily cleared his throat. He had reason to be nervous: Ellis was behind him out of sight with a gun in his hand. "Well, all I know, Arnie, is that he walked down through. They do that sometimes, you know. . . . Where the hell is the marshal?"

Arnie was watching the alley doorway when he replied. "I don't know. He ain't been around since night before last as near as I've heard."

The liveryman glanced toward the alley. There was no one

in sight. He surprised Ellis by saying, "He's out there, Arnie," and started down the runway. Arnie followed him, passed the harness-room doorway and got about fifteen feet southward when Ellis stepped out and called him. "Cowboy!" The posseman stopped dead still. "Turn around, cowboy!"

The man shuffled his feet, then faced Bowman with an expressionless look. Ellis pointed his gunbarrel low. "Toss the gun away. . . . Good. Now walk into the harness-room and don't be foolish or I'll overhaul you."

Arnie glared at the liveryman, who waved his arm defensively. "What the hell was I supposed to do? He was behind me with a gun."

Arnie said nothing. He marched into the harness-room and halted without facing around. He might be furious but he was not foolish. Ellis stopped briefly in the doorway, then holstered his weapon and started forward. Arnie did not have a chance. He was as tall as Bowman, a few inches taller in fact, but he lacked forty pounds of being as heavy and was nowhere nearly as powerfully strung together. Still, he raised his hands as Ellis closed on him, and batted away the left-hand fist, which was what most men would have done, and which was a mistake, because the right fist came at him from shoulder height and Arnie went down atop a pile of salt-stiff old smelly saddleblankets.

The liveryman was unable to move out of the doorway or to speak. He watched the burly stranger tie Arnie swiftly and efficiently, as though he had been tying a calf, and when Ellis arose the liveryman showed a sickly smile.

Someone was coming up the runway from the direction of the back alley. The liveryman turned his head as though to do so was painful.

Ellis edged closer to the doorway, but he had overlooked something when he had captured Arnie. A man stopped mid-way and spoke sharply to the badly upset liveryman. "What the hell. . . . Whose gun is that?"

The liveryman lowered his eyes to the gun Arnie had

dropped, flashed a mottled tongue around his lips and replied without hesitation but with a false ring to his voice that would not have fooled a child. "Mine, I guess it fell out'n my waistband when I was bringing this bay horse up here."

Ellis sweated until the man he could not see said, "What the hell are you doin' carryin' a gun in the mornin' when you're doing chores?" He picked the weapon up, turned it in his hand to gaze at it, and Ellis knew when he heard the sharp intake of breath, that he had recognized the weapon. Ellis gave the liveryman a powerful shove that sent him sprawling, and jumped ahead with his sixgun in hand.

The posseman's reaction was the right one: he started to steady the gun he had been loosely holding, but he was far too late.

Ellis snarled. "Drop it!" The posseman opened his fingers. "Now the other one!"

Just for a moment the posseman's eyes wavered in their regard of Bowman, then he very slowly lowered his right hand toward the hip-holster. He had his fingers atop the gun-grip when he stared steadily at the man in front of him, and once again instinct shrilled soundlessly in Bowman's brain, but it was too late. Someone cocked a Colt no more than fifteen feet behind him.

The man in front snarled. "Ease down the hammer," he instructed Bowman. "Real slow an' easy. . . . Now then, just let the gun drop."

This time the man he could not see and had not known was behind him, came soundlessly up and jammed the barrel of his weapon into Bowman's back.

Ellis let the gun fall.

The liveryman was upright again, covered with fragrant runway dust, shaking like a leaf and cowering in case there was gunfire.

Ellis and the lean, faded individual facing him regarded each other through a short interval of silence before the man whose gunbarrel was against Bowman's back said, "Ev, there ain't no moneybelt under his shirt."

Everett's bloodless lips pulled back in a menacing smile. "Well now, let's take him into the harness-room and make real sure of that." Everett drew his gun slowly and used it to gesture with as he said, "Walk, Mister Bowman, or whatever your name is."

Ellis walked. The liveryman pressed flat against a stall door upon the opposite side of the runway, and was completely ignored by the armed men. After they had entered his harness-room behind their captive, he bolted for the rear alley.

Ellis did not get a good look at the man who had come up behind him until the man saw their companion lying inertly atop the saddleblankets tied hand and foot. He turned on Ellis with a snarl but Everett gave a sharp order. "Just cut him loose, Judd." Everett was calm. As the unconscious man was being freed Everett said, "Where's the moneybelt, Bowman?"

"Locked in the jailhouse safe."

Everett accepted that. "Where's Will Thompson?"

"In the mountains."

"What's he doin' up there?"

Ellis's answer sounded believable. It should have; he had told the same lie before. "Keepin' watch over the eleven thousand dollars from the bank."

Arnie was freed of his ropes but he remained out of it. Judd straightened up looking intently at Bowman. His expression was eloquent but before he had a chance to speak Everett asked another question of Bowman.

"The bank money? How do you know that?"

"Because we both left town before daylight this morning. We rode up there together."

There was an implication to this statement that made Everett and Judd exchange a look. Everett said, "He knew where the loot was?"

"No, he didn't. I did. I saw that feller calling himself Sam Hanks down on his knees in some trees behind the cabin burying something."

Finally, Judd had a chance to speak. He looked dubious. "I'll be damned. Bowman, when did he learn where that money was hid?"

"Yesterday."

Judd frowned. "Ev, he double-crossed us."

But Everett was not that quick to condemn. "He never said a word to me about divvying anything, Judd."

"Well, he should have. He had plenty of time to tell us before he taken Bowman here and rode up there. After all, we been his friends for a long time. We rode ourselves raw with them damned cattle."

Ellis ventured a dry remark. "Friendship sort of gets lost sometimes when there's a lot of money lyin' around."

Everett agreed with that, and holstered his Colt. "That's a plain fact, Mister Bowman. . . . Well now, Judd, we can think about Will later. Right now I think we'd ought to take Mister Bowman up the back alley to the jailhouse and break into Will's safe."

Judd was slower than his friend. He looked fiercely at Ellis for a moment, then down at the unconscious man on the old saddleblankets, and finally at Everett again. "What about him?" he asked, pointing downward. Ellis thought Everett ran true to type when he offered an indifferent response. "He can lie there. He didn't do us no favor this morning; he liked to have got me shot, and after Bowman would have shot me he'd have shot you. . . . Judd, we don't have all day. . . . Bowman, turn around real slow and walk down toward the alley."

There was no sign of the liveryman and Ellis's bay ridgling cocked a bored eye as the three men left the harness-room walking past him. Judd stopped to retrieve the guns lying in the dust and because he only had one holster, with his own gun already in it, he stuffed one weapon into his waistband

and walked along carrying the other one. The first gun was the one Ellis had commandeered from Jake, and the second belonged to the unconscious Arnie back in the harness-room.

Everett's personality began to show itself to Ellis as they reached the alley and turned up it: He seemed to be imperturbable. Even when he had been facing Bowman's cocked sixgun he had not appeared afraid, and now, as they walked along, he wagged his head and quietly said, "We might have to settle for Bowman's money, Judd. . . . I'd lay big odds Will aint' nowhere close around at all, if he was left alone in them mountains with all that bank loot. . . . Bowman?"

"Yeah."

"How about the feller who stole that money; any sign of him up there?"

"He'd be a damned fool to show up after we'd found his cache. For eleven thousand dollars a man could shoot a bank robber and not be bothered much by his conscience."

Ev looked at Ellis with a dry twinkle, and continued to look at him until they were turning toward the back door of the jailhouse, but he remained silent.

Judd looked at the buckled door hasp with no padlock and scratched his head until Ellis said he had been here earlier. Then Judd pushed the door open without speaking and found himself nearly blind in the windowless storeroom. He thrust out an arm to feel for the second door, the one leading into the office.

Behind Bowman the lanky man spoke with sharp irritation to Judd. "Get the damned door open, will you, it's darker'n the inside of a boot."

Ellis reacted. Earlier, he too had felt helpless in this dark windowless room. He turned soundlessly on the balls of his feet, with Everett faintly backgrounded by sunlight, and brought his left forearm down across Everett's gun with all his strength. The gun was torn loose. It struck wood somewhere to the left as Ellis came across with his right fist, aiming for the face he could barely see. The shock of a direct hit rocked Ellis back on his heels. Everett was punched backwards. The edge of the partially opened door caught the posseman the full length of his spine. As he was sprawling, Ellis crouched low and sprang sideways. Judd, who was slower, tried a roundhouse strike but it was too late. He was off-balance from the violence of his swing when Ellis came under it and sank a fist wrist-deep into Jake's middle. As the battered man's breath burst outward, Ellis straightened up enough to hit him again, along the slant of his jaw this time, and felled Judd.

It had not taken ten seconds for the fight to begin and end. Ellis stepped across Judd to open the door leading into the office, and with more light he then went back to close the alley door, and to lean on it looking down.

While he was catching his breath and waiting for his heart to slow a little, someone rattled the jailhouse door from out front. He rattled it several times then went stamping away.

Ellis dragged his victims down into the cell-room, locked them both into the same cell he had occupied, and pocketed the big brass key. He had four handguns, decided to keep Jake Mitchell's weapon, tossed the others atop Thompson's desk and left the jailhouse the same way he had entered it.

There was a woman with red hair and a mouthful of clothespins hanging wash across the alley and a few doors northward. As Ellis emerged she saw him and stopped to stare. He touched his hat to her, closed the door and walked down the alley. The woman watched him until he was almost as far south as the liverybarn, then gave a little shrug and went back to her work.

# CHAPTER 13
# A Pleasant Ride

RIDING away from Batesville in broad daylight was both a relief and a cause for anxiety.

Anxiety concerning what he might find up ahead, and anxiety because of the hornet's nest he had stirred up in Batesville. Soon, the man he had knocked unconscious in the liverybarn, the liveryman, the banker, and only the Lord knew who else—including Judd and Everett—would be all fired up to get a piece of his hide.

But when everything else piled up on a man, if he had the disposition for it, he could look at a turquoise sky, at the far rims and peaks, at the lift and flow of natural beauty in all directions, and feed his soul.

Ellis looped his rawhide reins and rolled a smoke. His bay horse was happy to be out of a stall. It slogged along on a loose rein and later, when it got a little leg-pressure it was glad for the opportunity to lope for a mile or so.

Ellis looked back occasionally, but there was no one in sight. Once, he startled some deer resting in tree shade, perfectly camouflaged until they sprang up and ran. Another time, as he was nearing the low, rolling foothills on the east end of the big upland meadow, he came upon a badger and a bobcat in a Mexican standoff. The cat was faster, more agile, and also more careful. The badger feared nothing and made little snarling charges until the cat saw the horseman and gave up its quest for a meal.

As he was emerging on the far side of the foothills with the stand of sugar pines in view, it occurred to Ellis that the wisest course would not be to ride directly toward the glade and the cabin.

If all had gone well, Samantha should still be in charge, but with someone like Marshal Thompson one would never know, so he angled over closer to the barranca wall of Custer Meadow and made the ridgling pick its way among the loose rock and scratchy underbrush, which the horse clearly did not enjoy.

They got a fair distance northward before there were big trees to provide shade and cover. Ellis guessed they were about parallel with the meadow before he turned slightly in that direction, up where the timber was thick and close.

The horse picked up a scent before the man could see anything through the trees, and because the horse and the man had worked in tandem for enough years to complement one another, Ellis swung off, left the horse tied in shade, and went ahead on foot.

He came in from the west and passed through the foremost ranks of huge old trees with a clear view of the glade, the cabin, and horses in the corral out back dozing in sunwarmth. He hunkered like an Indian and did not move for fifteen minutes. Then Samantha came outside and flung a dishpan full of water out where the dust lay thickest in front, and paused to stand a moment, sorrel-blond hair glowing in sunlight like pale copper. She went back inside the cabin and Ellis arose to return to his horse. He mounted it and continued northward so that when he eventually emerged from the forest he was behind the cabin, which had no rear windows. He was seen at once by the dozing horses in the corral.

They watched and eventually one of them raised his head slightly to nicker. Ellis watched the cabin after that. He was within a hundred yards of the back of the cabin when something moving around the west corner of the cabin caught and held his attention.

It was Samantha carrying a carbine and with her old hat slanted down in front to shade her eyes. She stepped around the corner, holding the weapon with both hands poised to raise it instantly to her shoulder, when he laughed.

She did not lift the gun. Neither did she move until he was nearing the pole gate of the corral. Then she grounded the gun and said, "I hope you know you have given me gray hair."

He grinned and began hauling his outfit off the ridgling. As he knelt to hobble it because it could not be turned into the corral with the other horses, he said, "It wouldn't make a bit of difference to me whether you were gray or not."

He eyed the cabin. "Are they still tied up?"

She nodded her head. "Didn't you expect them to be?"

He halted facing her, still faintly smiling. "Yeah, I expected them to be—only with men like those two it don't pay to get too hopeful. An old man once told me I shouldn't trust anything that don't eat hay."

She snorted and although her expression was prim and faintly irritable, she sounded tremendously relieved as she said, "It's been the longest night of my life. . . . Are you hungry?"

"Always hungry, ma'am. But maybe if you think it's safe not to keep an eye on them for a few minutes, I could tell you a few things it'd maybe be just as well if they didn't hear."

She reassured him on one point. "It's safe. I tied them like shoats after breakfast this morning, and when they got to swearing, I stuffed rags in their mouths too. . . . I'm listening, Ellis."

He began with his fruitless ransacking of the Batesville jailhouse and ended with his departure from town after the storeroom fight and the locking of Thompson's two friends in jail cells. But what seemed to preoccupy her most was his recitation of the encounter with Charley Turner in the bank. She stared at the ground for a long time before raising her head to say, "He really doesn't know, does he?"

"Know what?"

"Who held up his bank."

Ellis studied her face for a moment before gently shaking his head. "I'd say he don't. Why should he?"

"Yes, he should. . . . Come inside and I'll feed you." She hesitated. "You shaved."

He nudged her and said nothing as they strode toward the doorway, but just short of it he stopped her with a hand on the arm, went silently around the west side of the cabin and with his gun in hand, looked in the window.

It was a fruitless precaution. The two men lying on the floor saw him and glared but both were so completely wrapped and tied they could do no more than roll.

He grinned, went back around in front and motioned for her to precede him inside. It was cool in the cabin. There was a tantalizing fragrance of recent cooking. He tossed his hat aside and watched her head for the hearth. She did not look around at him.

He went over beside Marshal Thompson, removed the gag, hoisted the big man until he was braced against the log wall, then told him how much money he had in the account down at Batesville's bank.

Thompson stared, then said, "Turner. I knew he was a blabbermouth."

Ellis ignored that to ask a question. "Didn't you get more than that for all those cattle?"

This time Will Thompson's bold glare swung away and did not return. "What the hell are you talking about? What cattle?"

Ellis looked past where Jake was listening to every word, then he spoke to the lawman again. "I locked Ev and Judd in the jailhouse. Arnie got in the way so I put him to sleep."

Jake stared. Ellis noticed this from the corner of his eye and continued in a conversational tone of voice. "They're sure you got the bank loot, Marshal. . . . Sooner or later someone is going to discover them locked up and turn them loose. . . . I told them you had the loot. I got the impression they figure you should divide it with them. Sure as hell they're goin' to track me to this cabin. If you don't have eleven thousand dollars on you—I don't think they'll believe you never had it."

Jake was straining against his ropes and making strangling sounds behind the gag. Marshal Thompson turned on him with anger. "Just shut up. Can't you see what he's tryin' to do—scare us."

Ellis arose and stood looking down. "You're wrong, Marshal. I'm not trying to scare you. I don't give a damn whether you believe me or not—but when Samantha and I ride out of here, you're going to stay."

Ellis went over where Samantha was piling food on a platter. She shot him a quizzical look, and when he was seated at the table eating, she leaned and whispered in his ear. "You're as devious as they are."

He looked up smiling. "I guess if you're goin' snake hunting you got to know something about snakes, don't you?"

After he had eaten he took her outside and around where the shade was. "I could sleep for a week," he said, then looked steadily at her. "Why did you rob the bank?"

"Because Sam Hanks made a will and gave it to my parents. I found it after they both died in a runaway. He left me his ranch and his livestock."

"What's that got to with robbin' the bank?"

". . . He also left me his money in the Batesville bank. The account book with the will said eleven thousand dollars."

"And?"

"And, I went to Charles Turner. He said he'd have to see the will, have it authenticated. When I agreed to bring it in, he also told me that Mister Hanks had no money in the bank and had never had an account there, and couldn't have made a will because he couldn't write."

"Maybe he didn't have money in Turner's bank."

She smiled icily. "Oh yes he did. I have the account book initialed by Charley Turner showing Sam had deposited three thousand dollars, the profit from his drives for the last three years of his life. It was with the will."

She eyed Ellis for a moment, then spoke with bitterness. "He had it and Charles Turner knew he had it. But Charles Turner did not believe there was a will. In fact, he told me twice that Sam Hanks could not write. That was a plain lie and I know it. Now you know why I asked if Charles Turner knew who had robbed his bank. He is a shrewd man. I took exactly eleven thousand dollars. No more and no less. I wanted him to know." She looked mildly puzzled. "I've been wondering about this ever since I shoved the barrel of my gun into the face of his clerk. Ellis, he is not a fool. He's got to know."

Ellis thought she was probably correct. But why hadn't Turner told Marshal Thompson? Why hadn't he cried out to the treetops the identity of the bank robber?

Ellis gave up thinking about that and reiterated what he had told her earlier about the old apothecary named Cuthbert. "That would make two witnesses. But that doesn't prove who killed Sam with his own branding iron—holding it wrong-side up when he hit him with it."

She moved in beside him where the shade was deepest and gazed steadily out across the little clearing. "I knew it. I've known it for years."

"How did you know it?"

"I felt it. I used to see Marshal Thompson up there. Not often and not always alone. And I never could catch him or get close enough to be absolutely sure. But I knew who it was and after Sam had died, I was more sure than ever." She paused to look at him. "Who was powerful enough to kill a man with a branding iron? You figured it out, didn't you? How many men in the Custer Meadow country are as physically powerful as Will Thompson?"

Ellis rubbed his jaw, which was beginning to get scratchy again. He knew very little about the law, beyond the basic fact that it authorized men with badges to lock up drunken cowboys and an occasional stage-robber; even horsethieves, if lawmen got to them first. And he knew, perhaps more by instinct than anything else, that there wasn't enough evidence to convict Will Thompson.

She had seen a very large man. She had said she had never gotten close enough to make a positive identification. He wagged his head at her. "I believe you, Sam, but I'm not the one you have to worry about. You got to convince a judge and maybe a jury about the killing."

"Ellis, it *was* murder."

He did not argue about that. "I expect it was. The old man who runs the shop of powders and whatnot down in Batesville thinks it was murder. But we're right back where we started. You and the old man can swear to how Sam Hanks was killed, but to get things straight for Sam Hanks you got to be able to prove who killed him. And you can't."

She was watching his face as he was speaking, her expression showing an out-of-character ferocity. "I'm not going to try to prove it," she said.

He interpreted that correctly and eyed her thoughtfully. "Sam, you can't just walk in there and blow his head off."

She did not answer. Instead, she settled back into the shade again and stood gazing across the meadow. Ellis watched her profile. Under different circumstances he would have smiled. She was as tough as rawhide, smart as a whip, pretty as anything he'd ever see come down the pike—and she was something else; a female version of the frontiersmen who carried the law with them—Judge Colt and his six jurymen.

He changed the subject. "They'll be trackin' me by now, Sam. At least Thompson's three friends; maybe more. There might be a whole posse of town riders. It's time we went somewhere else. Let them have Marshal Thompson and Jake. If it's a town posse they'll be after me and will most likely set Thompson free. If it's his friends—I got a feeling they might settle his hash because they think he got the bank money and double-crossed them. Either way, unless we take him along with us, they'll be riding into your meadow directly. If they find him I'd guess it might be about fifty-fifty that someone will shoot him."

"And if that doesn't happen?"

He reached to lay a hand lightly on her shoulder. "Sam, we've done an awful lot in the past day or two. Right now we both need a place to rest up, then figure out what's next, and standin' around this cabin isn't goin' to help us at all. Get your things. I'll go saddle the horses."

She did not argue. She straightened up and smiled. "I know the exact place."

He replied dryly. "I'll bet you do. If there's anyone in this country that knows hiding places, it's got to be you. Now go get whatever you need and meet me over by the corral."

He had no intention of giving her the initiative. Not because he would not want to go wherever she had in mind, but because he had an idea of his own.

# CHAPTER 14
## How Not to be Clever

ELLIS led the way up into the northward timber so the bound prisoners being left behind would not hear them departing. Then he maintained the lead by a very simple expedient: he reined in and out among huge trees in a way that would not permit her to ride beside him nor take the lead.

For a while she said nothing, but as they worked their way around the horseshoe curve of the forest above the glade and southward down along the east side, she finally said, "Ellis, turn due east and eventually we'll reach the stageroad."

He continued on around the meadow on the east side, riding south, and finally halted where he had an excellent view of the front of the cabin and the full expanse of the small meadow. Then he smiled enigmatically at Samantha and dismounted.

He expected indignation. What he got was an almost meek submission. She evidently had deduced on their ride around here that he had a purpose in mind. He led his horse farther back where it would also be unable to pick up the scent of other horses, and returned through forest gloom to an area of big trees and underbrush near the verge of the glade. He stamped down some wild grape to make a place of concealment. He watched her stamping underbrush and grinned to himself. He kept his back to her until they sat down, then explained. "I want to see who comes up here. If it's the marshal's friends, why then I expect that ought to be interesting, because if they find him tied up, he's going to have to talk like a Dutch uncle to convince 'em I didn't tie him and

Jake up, take the money and ran with it. Maybe they'll believe him, but either way it don't much matter—unless they get to poking around and find our tracks leading over here. In which case we'll have to either brush out our sign and keep ahead, or waylay them. Which idea do you like, Sam?"

She did not look like she really cared much for either suggestion. She said, "And suppose it's a big posse and not just Thompson's friends?"

His eyes twinkled at her. "In that case, we'll ride back and talk to them. They'd ought to be interested in the truth, don't you think?"

She was searching for reasons to find fault. Why she was doing this she would not have been able to explain even to herself. "And suppose Charles Turner is with a town posse?"

"I kind of like that idea, Sam. Providing it's not just the banker and the other ones, Everett, Arnie and Judd. If it's a real posse of townsmen, I think we can make someone believe us regardless of what Will Thompson has to say."

She turned to look out where there was sunshine and a deceptive aura of ongoing serenity. Then she looked back. "Mister Turner has a lot of influence in Batesville, Ellis, and among the stockman beyond town in all directions. No one crosses him."

He cocked his head at her. "Sam, you're tired."

"Yes."

"Lie back in the shade, put your hat over your face to keep gnats away, and sleep for a while. Don't worry, the moment I see anyone ride in, I'll waken you."

She ignored his suggestion and glanced southward toward the entrance to the glade again, then at the cabin, and her face softened. "I built that," she said, and quickly gave him a challenging look.

He nodded soberly. "I believe you, Sam. . . . Adzed the logs—everything?"

"Everything."

"That calls for a lot of heavy lifting."

She nodded. "Yes, but mostly it called for a lot of figuring how to use my horse and an old chain-block."

"Why? And why in this place?"

"Because I own the land. I inherited it from my parents. When I was small they would drive up for Sunday picnics. They loved it. They'd sit by the fire on snowy winter nights talking about the cabin they'd build up here someday."

He gestured. "And that's it?"

"Yes. Exactly the way they said they'd build it. But they didn't get the chance, so I did it for them. As a sort of memorial."

He turned to gaze at the cabin, marveling a little that a woman—a girl—as slight as she could have built it so well. He wagged his head and she saw him do that.

"Ellis, when you're not as big as Will Thompson you have to use your head to make up for the muscles you don't have."

He smiled. "You must have had some pretty big headaches from all that figuring. You sure did a fine job. . . . Samantha?"

"Yes."

"You love this country up around Custer Meadow?"

"Yes, very much. Do you like it?"

He answered slowly. "When I came out of the timber for the first time an' saw it,I thought it'd make about as nice a cow outfit as a man would ever want."

She regarded him through a period of silence. Then, whatever she might have said died in silence as she looked away from him. The sun was moving. Higher, up where the forest blocked out everything except the uppermost crags of pure granite where nothing grew, gray snow lay in crevices. That was the source for the creek that crossed Custer Meadow.

He decided she was not going to rest so he lay back, tipped down his hat and asked her to let him know the moment horsemen appeared in the glade.

She watched him get comfortable. He might have dozed

off but she suddenly spoke to him. "Why didn't Charley Turner tell Marshal Thompson about me robbing his bank?"

"Maybe he did."

"No. Marshal Thompson didn't know who it was until I removed my bandana. Then I am sure he made the connection. I am positive he didn't know who Sam Hanks was before. But I'm positive Charley Turner knew. Why didn't he tell the marshal?"

Ellis sighed in the blackness beneath his hat. "Do you ever sleep?" he asked.

She ignored the question. "I thought about that last night. Would you like to know what I came up with?"

"Sure," he said, and yawned prodigiously.

"Mister Turner doesn't want anyone caught for that robbery."

Ellis considered that for a long time in the darkness of his hat, then said, "Why not?"

"I don't know. But it has to be something like that. And what puzzled me is that as close as he and Will Thompson have been for years, Mister Turner was keeping my identity a secret."

"Maybe he's sweet on you, Sam."

She looked disapprovingly at the thick form with the hat over its face. She said nothing, but turned to lie bellydown and concentrate on the lower end of the glade.

Ellis lifted his hat with one hand and craned around to see her. "Did I hit a nerve, Samantha?"

She squared around. "That's foolish," she snapped. "Foolish and unwarranted. He's old enough to be my father."

"Samantha, there is many a good tune in an old fiddle. Did you know that?"

She raised up slightly and glared in his direction. It was wasted effort; he was back dozing again. Or pretending to.

While she was keeping watch, convinced he was asleep, he rolled over and propped himself on both elbows gazing at her. "Are you saying Turner won't turn you in for robbing his bank?"

"Well, he hasn't, has he?"

Ellis studied her a long moment, then nodded his head. "He's sweet on you, Sam."

She colored and glared at him. "That's ridiculous. I've known him since I was a little girl. Even after my parents were gone, he never once came to the house—well, once he did, two days after my father was buried, to tell me how sorry he was."

"And he never came back?"

"No!"

Ellis continued to gaze at her, but she would not meet his glance and faced forward again, sweeping the glade for signs of riders, of any kind of movement, and the next time he spoke she would not look around nor answer. He said, "I'll tell you something for a fact, Sam. You are mighty easy to look at."

Through an interval of icy silence which followed this remark, he sighed, settled back down in the wild grape and placed the hat over his face again. Then she turned and looked at him.

Fifteen minutes later she reached with a stick and poked him. He rolled over again. She pointed with the stick, so he sat up.

A solitary rider was sitting his motionless mount down near the lower end of the glade looking toward the cabin. He sat like that for a long time before reining back around and disappearing to the west.

Ellis sat up, scratched, watched for a long time, then made a guess. "They're not goin' to come right up across the meadow in plain sight. That was a scout. They're goin' up around the way I did. Most likely they're following my tracks. They'll come out up behind the cabin the way I did." He changed position so he would be able to see the curving long run of northward timber. She joined him in the vigil, and

once when he turned she met his gaze without either of
them saying a word.

He had made a good guess. They came out of the timber
riding Indian-file, one behind the other, aiming directly for
the corral. There were four of them. At that distance it was
not possible to make an accurate identification but Ellis was
sure the second to last rider was the man called Judd.

It was the last rider that held Samantha's attention. "The
one bringing up the rear is Charles Turner," she said.

Ellis switched his attention to the drag rider. He was not
completely surprised to know the banker had come up here
with those other men, but it seemed unlikely. Turner was not
an individual who would make a long horseback ride. The
bankers he had known, and a lot of other townsmen who
were merchants, never seemed very eager to go saddlebacking.

While the men from Batesville tethered their horses out
of sight of the watchers on the west side of the cabin, there
was nothing much to watch. Then when they came trooping
around to the front of the cabin, Ellis Bowman pursed lips.
Each one of them, including the banker, was carrying a
Winchester.

He softly said, "Sam, this ought to be interesting."

She did not respond. She watched the four men enter her
cabin. They were in there a long time. Much longer than it
would have taken them to cut Mitchell and Marshal Thompson loose, and later, when they emerged, not all of them
came outside. Mitchell was with the two men who did come
out. The three of them stood slightly apart studying the land
all around. They had a desultory discussion going on but
Ellis was much too distant to hear anything.

He wanted to see Marshal Thompson walk out into sunlight. Thompson and the banker and there was another man
inside with them. Ellis guessed it was probably Arnie, the
man he had knocked senseless in the harness-room.

Time was passing, Ellis got impatient but Samantha became apprehensive. The men out front ambled around out of sight in the direction of the corral. She said, "What are the other ones doing in my cabin?"

Ellis had no answer.

Samantha abruptly stiffened beside him. "They will ride up north and find our sign."

Ellis was not perturbed. He had thought they might do something like that. "We'll see them when they ride away from the cabin. Don't get upset."

One horseman did appear north of the cabin riding in the direction of the northward timber, and as he rode he leaned down the far side of his horse studying the ground. He was clearly following the tracks Ellis and Samantha had made when they had ridden away from the cabin.

Ellis watched this horseman for a long time with an increasing sense of uneasiness. For one thing the man was taking far too much time reading sign on his way up into the forest. For another thing he would occasionally sashay to one side or the other as though expecting to see additional tracks. A school boy would have known enough to stay on the fresh trail and not go riding helter skelter.

At the height of Ellis's uneasiness, Samantha touched his arm, then gripped it with an amazing degree of power for a woman. She did not have to say why she was digging into his arm.

Three men emerged from the cabin. One was easy to identify because of his massive bulk as Sheriff Thompson, even if he hadn't been rubbing his sore muscles and flexing his body. The second man had a paunch and Ellis said that one would be the banker. The third man was waving his arms angrily. He did not appear to intimidate Marshal Thompson at all, but the other man, the paunchy individual, seemed upset. It was not hot, but he was mopping his face.

Ellis made a guess. "They're talkin' about the bank loot."

Sam did not respond; she was concentrating on the large lawman.

Ellis repositioned his hat to shade his eyes. Both he and his companion were concentrating all their attention upon the men in front of the cabin, who were all gesturing now, acting angry.

"It'll be about money," Ellis said again, more dryly this time.

After a while Samantha turned to say something, and froze with her mouth open, looking back behind the place where they were lying.

A man she knew on sight was standing there with a sweaty shirt-front as though he had been trotting a considerable distance. She very gently said, "Judd . . . ?"

Ellis Bowman did not move. He continued to lie there watching the men over in front of the cabin and that rider up near the northward timber. He knew what had happened, what he had allowed to happen through unforgivable stupidity, and was so furious with himself that he did not even look over his shoulder until the man with the carbine simultaneously gave them an order and cocked his Winchester to emphasize that he meant what he said.

"Stand up real slow, both of you, and keep your hands pushed straight out in front!"

# CHAPTER 15
# Blood!

JUDD exchanged a long, unfriendly stare with Ellis.

"I ought to shoot you right here," he told Bowman. "If I don't, I got a hunch Will Thompson might, or Arnie. You give Arnie a wallop that's got his face swole bad. . . . All right, Miss Coe, you lead off. Walk out'n the trees straight across the meadow to the cabin, an' if either one of you bobbles, I'm going to shoot the cowboy here, an' brain you, Miss Samantha. . . . Just so's we'll understand each other. Now then, cowboy, you leave your gun behind among the grape bushes. You too Miss Samantha. . . . Now you two walk. Don't stop unless I tell you to. It ain't far and it ain't real hot."

They walked side by side, neither offering to break the silence. Judd would remember every word and would certainly repeat them.

Part way along Ellis felt for her hand and squeezed it. She squeezed back, then spoke to the man behind them. "Why are you doing this, Judd? My father was good to you when you needed work."

The answer she got was not unfriendly. It was just simply practical. "For money. Your paw helped me with little odds and ends, for a fact. Miss Samantha, I'm crowding fifty. Gettin' out of bed at some cow outfit in the dark at four in the morning, then workin' until dark when I could drop in my tracks. . . . Do you see any future in that?"

She did not respond and Judd did not speak again. Then he let go a rattling sigh. "There won't no harm come to you, Miss Samantha. . . . I don't expect I'd ought to say the same for that feller you're walking with. He caused me'n Everett an' Arnold a lot of grief down in town. If Mister Turner hadn't come and saw us locked in, an' broke us out, it would have been even worse."

Samantha eyed the position of the sun, then said, "Judd, the four of you couldn't ride out of town without a lot of people seeing you, and wondering."

But Judd was unworried. "Naw. Even if they wondered, what would that amount to? There are men ridin' in and out of town every day. . . . I'll give you some good advice, ma'am. Whatever the marshal asks you, tell him the truth. He's in a real bad mood and I've seen him do things when he's in that kind of a mood you wouldn't want me to tell you about. So just answer him straight out."

It was good advice, and like most good advice it went in its recipient's left ear and out the right. Samantha was glaring by the time Judd halted his captives about fifteen feet from Arnie with the discolored and swollen face and Marshal Thompson still having circulatory pains from being tied so long. The only man standing in front of the cabin who did not look exultant and fierce was Charles Turner. He looked worried.

The large lawman hooked thumbs in his shellbelt and glared from Bowman to Samantha Coe. He said, "All right. Charley just told me he knew who robbed the damned bank. Samantha, I come up here to find your cache. And I'm goin' to find it. . . . While we been watching you walk over here we come up with a pretty fair idea about how to make you tell us where the eleven thousand dollars is."

He leered and motioned for everyone to enter the cabin. Thompson was the last person inside. The room was crowded. Marshal Thompson muttered something to Arnie, who went immediately to the kindling box and proceeded to build a small fire. It blazed and crackled. Thompson said, "Arnie, you and Ev pull her boots off."

As those two men looked enquiringly from the lawman to the handsome woman, Arnie straightened back from the fire and spoke to Thompson. "Will, do his feet first. She won't be able to stand that. Besides, I ain't real strong on doing it to a woman."

Marshal Thompson turned on him and snarled. "You want to hear him scream because he cleaned your plow. . . . I'm after the damned money she stole. We'll overhaul him later. Now get her boots off!"

Everett, too, approached Samantha without looking at her face. But as Arnie and Everett started toward the captives Charley Turner got pale and looked away.

Ellis made a rapid decision. Even with the Winchester at his back he could not let this happen. He sprang forward. There was one second of excruciating pain, then blackness as he fell. Judd had anticipated something like this. Using his Winchester barrel as a club he dropped Bowman to the cabin floor.

Samantha's attention was diverted just long enough for Everett to seize her. The moment his hands were on her, she fought. She narrowly missed kicking Arnie as he came in, and he sprang away until Everett had tightened his grip on her. Then Arnie pulled closer. She could still kick, but Everett solved this by lifting her into the air until Arnie caught one flailing foot and clung to it. It required both men to wrestle Samantha to the ground. Even with one of them pinning her beneath his considerable weight, she fought them. Will Thompson laughed but no one else did, and Charley Turner looked almost ill as Arnie finally got both her boots off and flung them aside.

Judd leaned on his Winchester watching a thin trickle of blood make a scarlet streak down Ellis Bowman's cheek from the gash beneath his hat.

They pinioned her arms until Will provided them with his belt, then they secured both arms behind her back. She was rumpled, dirty, sweat-stained and fiercely defiant. She cursed Marshal Thompson. Jake, Arnie and Everett grinned and Charley Turner looked embarrassed. Will Thompson regarded the sinewy, handsome woman until she stopped struggling. Then he said, "It ain't really necessary, Samantha. And you'll beg me to let you tell me where that bank loot is cached—so why not tell me now? Then won't any of us have to go through this."

Before she could respond, Ellis groaned and groped along the floor with bent fingers. She looked across the floor, then up at Marshal Thompson again. "Help him. There is a bottle of whiskey in the cabin. Help him, Marshal."

Thompson also glanced down at the dazed man. "The whiskey's gone," he told her. "Jake, fetch a bucket of water and dump it over him. . . . Samantha—look." Thompson leaned and removed Bowman's hat. Where the scalp had been broken there was a mat of blood-soaked hair and a swelling that looked much worse than it was. Thompson held the hat aside while he watched Samantha's face go white. Then Thompson dropped the hat and smiled at her. "Listen to me. You think that's a bad wound? You got one minute to tell me where to find that damned eleven thousand dollars, then I'm goin' to hit him harder over the head, and maybe kill him."

Jake returned with half a load of water in a leaky wooden bucket which he upended over Bowman. The reaction was initially less than anyone seemed to expect. Bowman weakly coughed and lifted his head up from the soggy floor. For a while he did not move. When the others thought he was not going to move, he drew both arms in close and levered himself up into a sitting position. Without raising his face he gingerly explored the top of his head where the injury was, then gazed at the blood on his hand. Finally, he looked up.

Will Thompson was looking down, his face showing cruel amusement. Ellis turned his head very slowly to gaze at Samantha, then raised a hand in Everett's direction. Everett braced and pulled, then released the injured man's hand when Ellis was upright. He seemed fairly steady on his feet, but he looked terrible. Water-diluted blood plastered the shirt to his upper body, the water had caused his wound to start bleeding again, he had mud and grass stains on his clothing, and his eyes mirrored pure pain.

He made squishy sounds with his toes inside the boots where the water had seeped in and shook his head very slowly at this mild annoyance. He sat down on the floor and fumbled with his boots to empty out the water, and Thompson lost interest as did the others.

Thompson smiled at Samantha. "Time is up. Where did you put the loot, Samantha?"

She sneered at him. "You're going to steal it aren't you, like you stole Mister Bowman's money." She turned. "Mister Turner?"

He glanced at her, his color bad and his eyes darkly troubled, then he turned away.

Will Thompson laughed. "He ain't going to do anything. We already talked about that. Me'n Jake here, and Arnie, Judd an' Everett, we're going to divvy it all up. And then we're going to make a clean sweep of the bank down at Batesville after dark tonight. You got any idea how much money is in that bank, Samantha?"

She was staring at him with withering contempt and did not reply. His smile faded, his gaze hardened toward her, and he snapped out the order for his companions to carry her to the hearth, where his intention was to put one foot at a time into the flames until she screamed for mercy and told him where she had hidden the money. Ellis Bowman pushed himself around as though to arise—bolted up off the ground like an uncoiled spring, driving his body straight into Marshal Thompson. It stunned them all.

Someone squawked, probably Jake who was slow overcoming his astonishment and even slower fumbling to raise his Winchester. Will Thompson screamed and staggered away holding both hands to his middle where blood was seeping through. He stared in shock and disbelief at the bloody, dirty, bedraggled man standing in front of him holding the wicked-bladed bootknife in his right hand, the blade showing red, wet and shiny.

The moment of absolute astonishment lasted no more than a couple of seconds, then Jake lifted the carbine and Samantha kicked as hard as she could, dropping Jake to his knees strangling the screams of pain while hugging his groin with both arms. The Winchester lay forgotten in the turmoil.

Arnie's hand was gripping his leathered Colt when Everett said, "Gawd a'mighty," and stood transfixed watching big Will Thompson lose his fight to remain upright and sink with terrible slowness to his knees. The blood was spilling past his clenched hands as though he were striving to stop the flow and mend the terrible, deep slash by hand-pressure.

Everett's awed exclamation was only a slight diversion, but Ellis wheeled and threw the knife, and that was more of a diversion. Arnie jumped to avoid the knife and Ellis stepped in, grabbed Thompson's sixgun and was straightening up with it when Arnie recovered and lunged for his sidearm. He was fast, but not fast enough. Ellis fired from the hip; Arnie was punched violently sideways. Ellis steadied his aim and squeezed off another shot. That time Arnie went up off the ground from the massive impact and went over backwards, shot through the brisket.

Everett and Charley Turner were like stones. Turner probably had no sidearm or, if he did, it was not showing. But Everett was armed. He was also a tad slow with his reflexes, as he had demonstrated earlier when he could have raised his gun and did not do it. He seemed transfixed by the soaked, bloody man swinging a cocked gun in his direction while standing over Marshal Thompson who had begun to wilt further and slowly slide foward, face down.

Ellis gestured with the handgun. "Untie her," he rasped to Everett. "And dump that gun."

Everett obeyed like a sleep-walker. When Samantha was free she sprang toward Jake who was rocking back and forth in agony, still gripping his lower body and fighting back the urge to scream. She disarmed Jake, who seemed unaware of everything that had happened around him in the space of seconds.

Ellis let Thompson's sixgun hang at his side. He looked at Samantha with an increasingly hazy vision, then dropped without a sound.

She caught his sixgun and held it on Everett. Then she dropped down and eased Bowman over onto his back. He was breathing well, his eyelids fluttered and his hands occasionally jerked spasmodically. She raised a hand to push hair away and said, "Carry him to the wall bunk. And be careful with him."

Everett nodded without coming any closer as he studied the compact, heavy body of the man who had fainted. He was still looking down at him when he said, "Mister Turner, you'n Judd lend a hand."

The banker picked up Bowman's body by the ankles, Everett hoisted him with both hands under his arms, while Samantha stood to one side, her sixgun leveled. They made slow progress past her and very gently placed him on the wall-bunk. As they straightened up Everett looked at Charley Turner. "What happened to Will's gun—he was holding it."

"Dropped from his hand back there," stated the banker, and gropped for a handkerchief to wipe sweat off with. "Why?"

"Because," Everett said quietly, "I'm leaving."

Samantha's steely voice from the doorway said, "No you're not. Unless you want to go back to town tied across a horse the way your friends are going back." The sixgun pointed straight at him.

She leaned on the adzed fir log which served as the door frame. "Get some water from the hearth and wash his face and head. And be careful." As Everett obeyed, she crossed to one of the cupboards and opened it looking for the bottle of whiskey. She did not remember hearing Marshal Thompson say he and his companions had emptied it.

As Everett bent to wipe Bowman's face Samantha gave him another order. "Let Mister Turner do that. You go help your friend stand up. He looks awful. I didn't mean to kick him— that way—but I'm not sorry. Go help him."

Everett approached Jake but the moment he tried to help Jake arise, the injured man said, "Leave me be. I ain't ready to get up yet."

Everett pointed to the woman with the gun in her hand. "Come up slow, and lean on me, Jake. I'll get an arm around you."

Jake allowed himself to be raised to his feet. For the first time he saw Will Thompson and the great puddle of blood around him. His mouth dropped down; he seemed to have forgotten his own injury.

Everett tugged him toward a chair at the table in the center of the room. Jake also saw Arnie, face up with two slug-holes in him staring straight up at the ceiling. He would have missed the chair if Everett hadn't pulled him closer as he was sinking down.

The only man in the room who'd had an opportunity to do something was Judd, and he had frozen at the sight of the dying town marshal. Later, it was too late to do anything—Samantha was armed and in control.

# CHAPTER 16
# By Moonlight

THE day was dying. Samantha kept Everett busy. He had to drag Will Thompson and Arnie outside and roll them both into blankets. He then had to scrub the floor, but no amount of scrubbing would ever obliterate bloodstain from dry wood planking.

Jake's recovery was slow. Even when Samantha placed a bowl of barley soup before him, Jake shrank from exerting himself even enough to get the chair closer to the table.

Charley Turner sat staring out the window, his back to the others, and when Samantha took him a bowl of her barley soup, he scarcely more than shook his head and did not look at her. She took the bowl to the bunk, but Ellis was unable to do more than smile weakly. She did not believe his eyes were focusing yet, so she put the bowl aside and leaned to examine his scalp wound. It was an angry, swollen, matted mess. If she'd had scissors she could have cut the hair away. But she did get hot water from the hearth and washed the injury until it was possible to see the extent of it. Ellis was inert but fully conscious. He rolled his eyes toward her and said one word. "Bad?"

She forced a smile. "One time I fell out of an apple tree and skinned my knee. It looked worse. I'll feed you."

"No. Just water. What happened?"

Everett walked over and stood looking down as he said, "Where did you have that knife?"

"Inside my boot."

Everett went over to sit opposite Jake. He was not hungry either. Even watching Jake eat upset him, so he arose and went to stand in the doorway gazing out at the two rolled

**123**

blankets with dead men inside them. Everett acted as though he had lost any desire to take the initiative. Judd, too, was thoroughly demoralized.

Samantha lingered beside the bunk with someone's sixgun jutting from her waistband. She had hidden the other weapons under the bunk. She looked tired enough to drop. None of them looked much different, and when she finally stoked up the fire and closed the cabin door, Everett returned to the table opposite Jake and solemnly regarded his work-hardened hands. When Samantha asked him if he wanted some barley soup, he shook his head.

He said, "It all just fell apart. I told him—Jake—you was standing there when I told him, to forget about the extra damned money. There'd be enough without us trying to get that too. But no—you couldn't tell Will Thompson anything. . . . Feeling better, Jake?"

The weathered, lined face of the other man showed nothing as he nodded. "Yeah. What happened?"

Everett continued to study his callused hands as he replied, "Maybe tomorrow I'll tell you, but not now." He twisted to look in the direction of the bunk where Samantha was helping Ellis Bowman swing both legs over the side and sit up. Everett wagged his head, left the table, found an old blanket and made a pallet for himself in a corner of the room where he settled on his back looking straight up.

Ellis stumbled over to the hearth to wash his face, and as he straightened up from washing, he explored the lump on his head. Samantha handed him a small, rough towel and hovered as he dried himself. He smiled at her. The headache was still there but it was a lot less fierce than it had been. Finally, he ate some of her barley soup, and when he saw the way the banker was slumped, he raised a questioning gaze and Samantha shrugged and shook her head.

Later, when they had bound the wrists of Jake, Judd and Everett, and their ankles were lashed with belting-leather,

CUSTER MEADOW ■ 125

she took Ellis outside. A pale moon was rising, and the daylong warmth was beginning to depart.

He strolled to the corral with her and leaned there gazing in at the horses. "Sam, tell me something—where *is* that darned money."

She did not even hesitate. "You were lying on it. It's sewed into that grass mattress on the bunk."

He turned and gazed at her.

A soaring, soundless owl cruised past so intent on his nocturnal rodent hunt that he did not see the pair of two-legged creatures at the corral.

"Give it back, Sam," Ellis said quietly while watching the horses.

"All right."

He sighed. "It's goin' to make quite a sight tomorrow when we ride into Batesville with their town marshal face down across that big horse he rides, and the other one—Arnie—and two others for the jailhouse."

"And Mister Turner. Ellis?"

"What?"

"There is something wrong with him."

"Yeah. Well, I don't expect too many bankers see one man knifed to death an' another man shot in one day, and—"

"It can't be just that, Ellis. Even before the fighting started he looked as though he had aged ten years. Didn't you notice how—morose, or something like that—he was?"

Ellis had noticed something, but he had thought it was simple fear. "Scairt out of his wits," he told her.

She did not accept that. "Frightened, yes, but after it was all over, he seemed even worse."

Ellis was tiring of this topic so he said, "It'll take a while to get back to feelin' normal, I expect."

"Yes, I suppose so. I think I know a way to make the time go faster."

"Is that a fact? How?"

She raised one booted foot to the bottom-most peeled log

stringer and, looking in at the horses, told him her idea. "Go up to the meadow. . . . We could use the rest of the year rebuilding the log house up there. Add on a room or two. Hollow out some saplings and pipe water into the house. Split sugar pine shakes for the roof. . . . And maybe, if the weather holds, put together a new set of log corrals."

He looked at her but she would not face him. He felt the top of his head, then dropped the same hand to one of the poles. "That's all?"

"No. Burn slash, maybe. That'd be warm work in the fall of the year. Maybe even rack up some cordwood."

He sighed loudly. "Sam, this didn't just come off the top of your head, did it?"

"No. While I was building the cabin down here I'd lie awake at night thinking how, someday, I'd build a nice house up there, with water coming into the kitchen, and maybe make a big rock fireplace and. . . .

"You're a slave driver, Sam."

"No. I just love Custer Meadow, Ellis. I can see it as it should be, as I know it can be. It could be the best mountain ranch in the whole territory. It has everything."

He agreed with her, and he knew more about what was required of the land to make that kind of an outfit than she did. But all this was more or less idle talk meant to get a lot of unpleasant things out of their minds.

As they started back she nudged him. "What are you thinking?"

He gazed in at the horses when he answered. "To start with, you'd need a team of big, stout young harness horses. Then you'd need money for the nails and tools and all. And finally, what you'd need most would be an awful lot of muscle. And Sam, I think it's too late in the year to do all of it."

"Ellis, will you work for me?"

He stared at the horses thinking. "Sam, I never hired out

to a woman in my life. Anyway, I was just passing through this country."

"You could be the boss, Ellis. . . . If you were just passing through, where did you expect to stop?"

He had no idea. "Somewhere," he told her vaguely. "Just about anywhere that it don't snow three feet every winter and stay cold until July. Then commence getting cold again in September.

"Then you don't want to work for me; you want to ride on?"

"Did I say that, Sam?"

Her eyes flashed with exasperation but in the poor light he did not notice. "No. I was asking you a question."

". . . Just don't expect too much," he cautioned her. "It's autumn. Even in a country where the snow don't come early, it's the wrong time of the year to start things and expect to complete very many of them."

"Ellis—just answer my question: Will you help me? Will you work for me?"

"Yes'm."

She still clung to his arm, apparently unsettled by his abrupt answer.

She was about to say something when she suddenly looked southward. "Do you hear horses?"

He listened. It was a faint sound, occasionally louder than at other times, but she was absolutely right. Someone was approaching the glade. He said, "Who'd be riding in the damned dark?"

She was as surprised and baffled as he was, but she was also leary. "We'd better get inside."

They walked briskly until they were under the front over-hang with the door at their backs, then halted to listen again. This time it was easier to discern the sounds of shod horses on gravel in the night air.

"Three," he told her. "Maybe four. Who would it be?"

She did not know but she was uneasy about them—whoever they were—arriving in the night.

Inside, Charles Turner was asleep on the floor beside his chair. Jake snored but Everett's eyes were open when they entered. He watched Ellis drop the *tranca* behind the door into its steel hangers, then stand like a statue listening. Everett's interest quickened but he did not move in the gloom. Not until Samantha went to the hearth to make coffee and armed Ellis Bowman with one of the Winchesters she had hidden under the bunk. Then Everett slowly sat up and was about to speak when he, too, heard the oncoming riders. He elbowed Judd awake.

# CHAPTER 17
# Mysterious Horsemen

THERE was a coal oil lamp but Samantha did not light it, and because the moon was late it was darker inside the cabin than it was outside.

Ellis lifted the door-bar and opened the door a fraction, not to see but to hear. There was no sound. Whoever those riders were, they were no longer approaching the cabin. At least they were not doing it on horseback. He closed the door, replaced the *tranca* and watched Everett hunching as best he could with bound legs and wrists, squirming his way into a position so that he had a wall at his back. Everett said, "Who did you see?" He sounded a little hopeful even though he probably had no reason to be.

"No one," Bowman replied.

"But they're out there?"

Ellis answered dryly, "Yes, they're out there. Who would they be? More of Thompson's friends?"

Everett leered at him. "They could be."

Ellis eyed the other man in cabin-gloom. "You better hope they're not," he said, and went over to the stove for a cup of black coffee. Samantha watched him but remained silent. All the initiative seemed to have fallen on Bowman. There were a few obvious things; one of them was that whoever those men were out in the night, they'd had late afternoon sunlight to follow tracks up here. Another thing that puzzled him was the reason those men were out there. Did they know Samantha had robbed the bank, and were they up here to find her cache, like Thompson had been? Were they even from Batesville?

He finished the java, put the tin cup aside and went to the

window in the west wall to listen. To open the thing would have made noise. So far, to the best of Bowman's belief, the mysterious horsemen did not know anyone was in the cabin, unless, of course, they had smelled or seen smoke from the stove on the hearth.

The surest way to get some answers was to slip out while it was still dark, before the moon arrived, and see if he could find at least one of those strangers.

The moment that notion entered his mind he knew Samantha would fiercely oppose it. He looked over at her near the hearth. She was watching him as impassive and motionless as an obedient squaw. He grinned in spite of himself. Samantha Coe was unique: she was naturally forceful, determined and capable, but she could also be quietly subservient and unobstrusive. He shook his head and went over to her by the hearth and said, "I'm going out. Bar the door after me and stay alert."

She seemed ready to argue but she said nothing.

Everett watched them in silence. When she had allowed Ellis to slip out into the darkness and eased the door closed after his departure, Everett said, "That man's got more guts than brains." She ignored him.

The moon was rising, but on the far side of the cabin it was still very dark as Ellis worked his way toward the rear of the building. The only shelter, aside from patches of darkness, was near the corral, but he did not go over there; the horses would have thrown up their heads at any movement and that would have interested any two-legged watchers.

He knelt, leaned on his Winchester, and waited for sounds. It was a long wait, but eventually there was the sound of a snapping stick from the forest north of the cabin.

Ellis slid lower to the ground and waited.

When the moon arrived it splashed ghostly light in all directions except on the east side of the cabin and along its back wall. Northward, it showed faintly upon gray metal in a dull and reflectionless way. Ellis watched. When the faint luminous glow faded he knew there was a man up there. What bothered him more was the probability that there were several others somewhere around, and he had only seen moonlight glow off the dark steel of one man's carbine.

He could not leave the darkness of the wall now that there was moonlight. The blur of a man up along the foremost tier of big trees reappeared, but more easterly this time, and for a long while the man stood in motionless silence studying the rear of the cabin where there was no window or door.

Ellis made a guess. That one was weighing his chances of leaving the cover of big trees to cross open grassland on his way to the house. Where then were the other men? They could be doing the same thing from different directions. Evidently they had worked out a strategy which seemed to be based upon each man operating independently. The man Ellis was watching finally edged clear of the timber. It still made a perfect backdrop for him, but once he got far enough southward to be in watery moonlight, it was easier to see him.

He was a sturdy individual slightly more than average in height. He was wearing a riding coat that brushed his knees and he was staring straight at the back of the cabin so that if Ellis moved at all, the man in the coat would see him. Ellis eased down until he was flat out in the tangled grass, keeping his carbine behind him in the shade of the cabin wall. The moonlight that had reflected off the stalker's weapon could betray Ellis the same way.

The man had a measured stride. The closer he got the more he seemed to be resisting an urge to get out of the moonlight by hurrying. Ellis watched, waited, and made a judgment. Whoever the man was, he had very good control. Maybe he was a townsman but Ellis doubted it.

He could have shot the stranger any time after the man was highlighted by moonlight. But Bowman, too, had excellent control.

A night bird called from the dark west side of the meadow.

If it was not a night bird it was the best imitation Bowman had ever heard.

The oncoming stranger was getting close, and Ellis could not prevent the man from seeing him once he was near enough to look down into the rank grass. Ellis felt in back for his carbine, lifted it inches above the ground and with agonizing slowness brought it around. The stranger was still coming, his stride resolute and quiet.

Ellis got his body angled so that the gun-butt settled perfectly into the curve of his shoulder, then he began to raise the barrel an inch at a time. The stranger was now less than a pistol shot away and still walking, but now he brought up his carbine and held it across his body, ready for instant use. Ellis could not see a sidearm but felt sure the man had one. His loose old riding coat could have concealed two sidearms.

Ellis picked a place in moonlight and grass beyond which he could not allow the stranger to pass, and waited, Winchester ready, eyes fixed upon the man.

Finally, when that night bird shrilled again, the stranger looked to his right and faltered in his stride, but only for a moment. Then as he was facing forward to continue his walk to the rear of the shack, Ellis came up very slowly, like a coiled snake, and cocked the Winchester.

The stranger saw him, heard the unmistakable sound of steel over steel and made no move to swing his own Winchester to bear. Whatever else the man was, he was not a fool.

Ellis spoke in little more than a whisper. "Just keep coming, and let the carbine hang in one hand at your side. No noise, mister. Come ahead."

The man obeyed to the letter. He had a trimmed beard, which had not been noticeable earlier in the moonlight because the hair was gray.

Ellis said, "That's close enough. Now then—ease the carbine down to the grass. . . . Good. Now the gun under your coat, and if you think you can beat a gun cocked and aimed at you, go right ahead and try it."

The stranger dropped his handgun. Perhaps because he felt safer now that he was unarmed and therefore not subject to being shot, he said, "Who are you?"

Ellis got to his feet. He and the stranger were about the same height, and fairly close to the same heft, with Bowman having the slight edge. In age, though, they were separated by several years. Ellis's captive was probably in his late forties or fifties. It was hard to tell in the moonlight.

Instead of answering the older man's question, Ellis asked one of his own. "Who are you?"

The answer was direct and immediate. "U.S. Marshal Craig Moore."

Bowman gazed at his prisoner. "Is that a fact? What are you doing up here?"

"Lookin' for a man."

"Bank robber?"

Craig Moore nodded very slowly without taking his eyes off Ellis Bowman or speaking. Moore obviously thought he had found his man.

Ellis changed the subject. "Where are your friends?"

"By now I'd say they're in a surround position."

"How many are there?"

"Three counting me."

Ellis's teeth shone in a wry smile. "Three men got this meadow surrounded?"

The older man relaxed, hooked thumbs in his shellbelt and studied the powerfully muscled younger man. "Mister, you don't need an army. Three good rifle-shots can cover every door and window in that shack. That's all it takes. No one comes out or goes in, and when you run out of water and grub, we'll still be waiting. . . . Mind telling me your name?"

Ellis did not mind, but he did not answer; he eased off the carbine hammer, grounded the weapon, and gazed at his prisoner. "Empty your pockets," he said. "Put everything into your hat. If you're carryin' a belly-gun, my advice to you is not to try and use it. Now empty them!"

The man calling himself Craig Moore obeyed as exactly as he had obeyed other orders. When he had everything in his hat he held it out. Ellis shook his head. "Put it down in the grass, then walk back twenty feet."

Moore did as he had been ordered to do, then he stood with what must have been an habitual stance, thumbs in shellbelt, expressionless, bearded face composed, and watched Ellis retrieve the hat and paw through its personal property until something pricked his finger and he risked looking down, and that was when Craig Moore sprang.

He covered the distance between them with three bounds and was swinging a gloved fist as Ellis raised his head, and jumped desperately sideways. He dropped the Winchester and the hat as Moore came after him with the speed and ferocity of a mountain lion. Ellis braced into the attack, warded off a strike and countered, but Craig Moore did not give ground. He twisted, ducked and twisted back, his arms darting in and out. He seemed to be enjoying what he was doing. Very soon Ellis Bowman learned that the older man was very good at this. He hit Ellis three times to each blow Bowman landed, then he began maneuvering Bowman toward the log wall of the cabin.

Ellis used superior weight to force the older man away, but Craig returned, weaving and pawing. He could sting but he could not put Ellis down. When a knotty fist came over Bowman's raised left arm and caught him flush on the jaw, a horde of tiny multicolored lights exploded in front of Ellis's eyes. Instinct told him to cover up and dodge sideways along the log wall, which he did, but the older man never let up.

Ellis shoved his left arm out to keep Moore at that distance, turned slightly to one side, pulled back his right, and as Moore came in, Ellis caught him over the heart with his cocked right fist.

Moore was stopped stone-still. His arms dropped and his jaw sagged. Ellis punched another blow over the heart and that time Moore's legs wobbled, but instinct took over. The older man back peddled, and bobbed left and right forcing Ellis to miss three times in a row. Moore needed time for his recovery, and fast though it was, it left his timing off and his reflexes sluggish. Even so, he caught Ellis in the middle with his left hand and grazed his temple with the right fist.

Ellis stepped back to suck air and study the older man, then he slammed forward with both arms up, body crouched, and used his weight more than his skill to force Moore away along the wall, until his boot-heel caught Ellis's carbine in the grass. When that happened Moore tried to step clear of the weapon and Ellis rushed him. Moore struck him twice in the body and was getting his feet untracked when Ellis overpowered him, closed oaken arms around the older man, locked his hands and exerted pressure, continued to exert it until Moore's breath exploded outward. He rained futile little blows but Bowman buried his face in the older man's shirt, ignored the light strikes of the desperate older man, and regripped his hands in back and strained until the muscles of his neck stood out. Then he abruptly released the older man and stepped back to let Moore fall at his feet, conscious but just barely, gasping for gulps of night air.

Ellis leaned, shoved Moore flat on his back, and with one knee in the older man's stomach, held Moore to the ground. Ellis cocked a big fist. "You had enough?" he asked.

Moore bobbed his head, still trying to get air.

Ellis got off him, yanked the older man to his feet and slammed him hard against the log wall and held him there. "If you make a move, mister, I'll break your damned neck." Moore did not move. "An' if you lie to me again, I'll do worse. Now then—who are you and who are those bastards with you?"

"I told you. My name is Craig Moore. I'm a U.S. marshal. Those men with me are also U.S. lawmen."

"Where is your badge?"

"In my hat."

Ellis continued to grip the older man by the throat and lean on him. Moore's face was getting faintly red. Ellis swung the older man and sent him sprawling in the grass near his hat. He leveled a finger. "You put your nose in the dirt and don't move."

Moore rolled belly-down as Ellis knelt to rummage in the hat, and once again, something sharp pricked his hand. He groped for it, raised it to the moonlight and stared at it.

The object was a small concave steel circlet with a star inside it and a legend around the circlet, barely visible, which said, United States Marshal.

Ellis let his breath out slowly. He was still not convinced. "Roll over and sit up," he ordered. When the older man was sitting up Ellis held out his left hand with the badge on its palm. "Where did you steal this thing?"

Moore was still breathing hard but, otherwise, he seemed to have recovered. "I'll tell you something, mister; you're the most pigheaded man I've ever run across an' I been at the law business going on twenty years. . . . I didn't steal that damned badge. I was sworn into my job and given that badge, and this time I'm lookin' for you—the feller who robbed the Batesville bank—only you sure don't much act like a banker."

Ellis gazed at the older man still with his left hand held out. "A banker?"

"The banker who robbed the bank down at Batesville. That's who we came into this damned country to take into custody, and you still don't look like a banker to me. You sure don't fight like one."

Ellis tossed the badge back into the hat, got comfortable on the ground facing the older man, and worked his aching right hand as he said, "Talk, mister."

"All right. Your name is Charles Turner, isn't it?"

"No it's not. My name is Ellis Bowman."

That made Craig Moore blink and hesitate for a long moment before he began speaking again. "Do you know Charles Turner?"

"Yeah."

"Where is he?"

Ellis jerked a thumb. "In the cabin."

"I'll whistle up my friends and we'd like to go inside and see for ourselves."

"You don't whistle up anyone, mister, until you explain what this is all about."

# CHAPTER 18
# The Enlightenment

ELLIS Bowman could have believed almost anything but what he heard from the federal lawman.

It was not actually a complicated story, but it most certainly was an unexpected one. "In the first place," Moore stated, "what got us interested in Denver was the counterfeit money. There was a lot of it and it was showing up all over northern New Mexico and southern Colorado. We got several hundred dollars worth of it so we could make comparisons. It all came from the same plates; each fifty had the same hair-line imperfections. So—three of us came down here to spread out and ask around. We came together in Batesville. That was the end of the trail. The town was full of it, an' it all came from one place, Turner's bank in Batesville. So—we went after Turner about the same time we got told that him and the town marshal and some other fellers left town together heading into the mountains. It wasn't hard to sort through the tracks and find the freshest ones that came up this way. We—"

"Wait a minute," Ellis said. "Counterfeit money? That don't make a whole lot of sense. Why the hell would a bank with plenty of cash deposits go into the counterfeit money business?"

Craig Moore showed a bitter smile when he replied. "Are you a rancher?"

Ellis nodded.

"I'm not," stated Moore, "so I know for a damned fact you could tell me things about the livestock business I never would have imagined. . . . I'm a law officer, a federal law officer; we get sent out on some of the damnedest assignments you would ever imagine. Why did Turner counterfeit money? Mister, I don't know whether it's happened exactly like this before or not, but I can prove to you, if we ever get down to Batesville, how it happened this time, because we got his clerk locked in the Batesville jailhouse. . . . Turner—I don't know yet where he got those counterfeiting plates— began making counterfeit fifties and hundreds. When he'd have maybe four or five thousand dollars' worth he'd slip it into the bank's reserve—and remove the same amount of money that was not counterfeit. According to his clerk, he'd send the good money to some bank up in Denver to a personal account. We'll go after that when we get back up there, but right now every large note in the Batesville bank is counterfeit. Turner was robbing his bank better than anyone could have robbed it using a gun—but it's still bank robbery."

When the federal officer finished speaking, he sat watching Ellis Bowman's expression, and eventually he smiled. "Did he get some of your money too?"

Ellis shook his head. "Did you know his bank was robbed by a gunman?"

Moore nodded. "Yeah, but not until a few days ago when we all met in Batesville and the barman told us." Moore's grin widened. "Somewhere, there is an outlaw with saddlebags full of worthless money."

Ellis glanced past the older man at the cabin's rear wall. Quietly, he told Moore about Will Thompson, who was rolled in a blanket around in front of the house, and how he had found Ellis and taken his money. Then he said, "But Turner told Thompson my money wasn't the money taken from the bank—why would he do something like that? Hell, he could have kept his mouth shut and maybe got it away from Thompson—although I sure wouldn't have wanted to have to bet the money on that. Thompson was after my money, and I had to weasel around to beat hell to keep him from getting it. Now—why would Turner refuse to take my money?"

Craig Moore shrugged. "If you're ready, we can go inside and ask him. . . . Mind if I whistle to my partners?"

Ellis gazed a long time at the older man in silence. It was not the badge that finally convinced him to nod his head, it was the story Moore had just related: No one could make up something like that on the spur of the moment.

"Go ahead. Tell them to come around on the back side of the house."

Craig Moore raised his head and whistled a night-bird call that was absolutely believable. Almost at once he got back two replies, one from the northwest, the other from the northeast.

Moore settled down to wait, and studied the younger man who had whipped him. He still ached from the bear-hug, and he was sore in other places from big, hard fists, but most of all he was interested in Bowman's puzzlement.

"Turner didn't act normal, even before Thompson and one of his friends got killed. Afterwards, he sat staring at the wall and didn't even eat. Sam said something was wrong with him. I thought he was sick—or maybe upset because of the killings. Did he have any idea you were on his trail?"

Moore doubted it. "I don't know about that, but just before we left Batesville to come up here we sat in the saloon and did some guesswork. One thing we did know because his clerk told us: Charles Turner sold his house and had cashed in everything he had, and he kept the money in a locked box in the bank safe. What does that sound like to you, Mister Bowman?"

"Like he was gettin' ready to run for it."

"Yeah. That's what we figured, which was why we decided not to wait, and started out to run him down."

Ellis eyed the older man. "Can you tell the good money from the bad money?"

"Yeah. But it takes a strong magnifying glass to do it."

"Do you have that kind of a glass with you?"

"I don't, but Wes Logan, one of the fellers who came up here with me has one. Why?"

"Because, Marshal, that eleven thousand dollars that was taken at gunpoint from the bank is inside the cabin."

Moore's expression changed. "For a fact?"

"Yes."

"Where?"

"Sewed inside the canvas cover of the straw mattress on the wall-bunk. I'd like to know whether it's counterfeit or not."

Moore's stare was direct. "How did it get into the mattress cover?"

Ellis was unwilling to answer that. "I'll tell you later. If you fellers know where Turner weaseled away the good money up in Denver, can you impound it and see that it gets sent back down here so's the folks who own it can get it back?"

"Yes. But it's got to go through a law court and the bank's depositors got to have written proof about how much of it belongs to them. Those things take a little time. Maybe a month."

A night bird sounded in the timber north of the cabin. Moore answered it—twice—which was evidently the signal for the men up yonder to approach the cabin. Ellis watched them emerge from forest blackness and walk out into watery moonlight. Both had Winchesters, both had those long riding coats, and one of the men was a head shorter than the other one.

Moore got to his feet, waited until he knew the approaching men could see him, then waved them on in. Beside him, Ellis Bowman picked up the carbine he had lost in the grass, examined it briefly, then put it in the bend of his arm as the other two strangers came up and halted, looking from their companion to the muscular man standing beside him.

Moore did not mention the fight but got right to the point by repeating everything he had learned from Bowman. He did not even introduce his companions until the shorter man shoved out his hand as he said, "Wes Logan, Mister Bow-man." The taller man also offered his hand and introduced himself. "Frank Huddleston. . . . How many folks are inside the house, Mister Bowman?"

When Ellis named Samantha Coe, all three men stared at him. They had obviously not expected a woman to be here. When he named Judd, Charles Turner, then Everett, and explained about the brace of dead men around front, the shorter man looked Ellis up and down. "You been busy," he said. "About this lady, Mister Bowman—how does she come to be here?"

"For one thing she owns this glade and the cabin. For another thing she's the heir of an old gent named Sam Hanks who owns that big meadow up yonder. . . . It's kind of a complicated story. Maybe, after you gents have talked to Turner, we can discuss the other things."

Craig Moore was staring. As he had explained, he had been in the manhunting business for many years. A keen and quick recognition filled his face. He said, "The lady robbed the bank at gunpoint."

It was less a question than it was a statement. His friends stared at him with as much interest as Ellis showed. Moore smiled. "She owns the cabin, so she'd head for it. Mister Bowman, in all my years runnin' down outlaws, I never once knew one that could sew, or who hid his loot inside a mattress. . . . Before we go inside, I'd like to hear what you know about why she held up the bank."

Bowman let out a long, silent breath while gazing at the perceptive law officer. He finally said, "All right. But first— when we go inside you're not goin' to tell her any of this. You're goin' to leave her alone. Is that understood?"

Moore nodded without taking his direct, keen gaze off Ellis Bowman. "All right. We'll say nothing—now. But when we get back to Batesville you got to understand we get paid to do a job, and that includes talkin' to folks who use guns to rob banks."

Ellis had to settle for that. He told them about the murder of Sam Hanks, about the missing livestock, and the sudden affluence of Marshal Will Thompson. He explained how Sam Hanks had died—with the clear imprint of a big horseshoe in his face, upside-down. And how Samantha got exactly even, no more, no less, after Charles Turner denied that Hanks had an account or had left a will. Now, it was the time for the lawmen to look intrigued.

Craig Moore said, "Wes can look at the money, but Mister Bowman, sure as we're standing here, it's counterfeit. If she only took it last week that was long after Turner sent all the good money up north, and was using the counterfeit money across the counter." Moore reflected before saying a little more. "I've gone after counterfeiters before, and I got to tell you I've caught damned few, but then those other fellers never stayed in one place, and Turner did. Not only stayed, but played a very dangerous game by handing out his counterfeit money to local folks who put a demand on him."

The marshal spoke laconically. "Of course he was a damned fool to get started with something like counterfeiting, but we know he was poised to run for it, so maybe the really stupid thing he did was let the marshal dragoon him into riding up here. They get hunches about when to cut and run."

Moore glanced around, then back. He was clearly getting impatient. He addressed Bowman crisply and matter-of-factly. "We'll follow you around front, Mister Bowman. It's not that we don't trust you, but you said Turner is in there along with three of Thompson's fake possemen. I been at this business a long time. The reason I'm still around is because I don't walk into ambushes. You understand?"

Ellis eyed the older man with hard amusement in his gaze, but he said nothing. Eventually, before this mess was finished, Marshal Moore would discover that the people who might try to ambush him were no longer able to do any such a thing.

He led the way. The moon had shifted considerably. Bowman realized he had no idea how long he had been occupied around behind the cabin. What had seemed to mark a passage of perhaps half an hour, had in fact marked the passing of several hours.

The federal lawmen stopped in their tracks at the sight of those cocoonlike objects in front of the cabin. One of them, the shorter man, went over to pull back blankets and gaze at the corpses. As he straightened back around he looked at Craig Moore and said, "Deader'n rocks," and walked back.

Ellis rapped on the barred door. Instantly, a muffled tenor voice demanded to know who was out there.

Ellis replied. "Me—and three federal marshals. It's all right, Sam."

She opened the door with a sixgun in her fist. The lawmen stood motionless until Ellis reached gently to push the weapon aside. Then he pointed to each lawman and named them in turn.

Samantha nodded and abruptly turned away to do something that had been bothering her since sundown. She did not like darkness so she lit the coal-oil lamp and put it on a shelf near the hearth.

Light dissolved darkness. It showed three bound men along the west side of the front wall, and another man, not tied and slumped on a chair with his hands between his legs.

# CHAPTER 19
# Someone's Mistake

CHARLES Turner listened to what Marshal Craig Moore had to say without once straightening up on the chair or raising his eyes; but Jake and Everett, over by the front wall, listened intently. When Marshal Moore paused to fish a folded warrant for Charles Turner from inside his riding coat, Jake turned to stare at Everett, who returned the gaze, but with much less astonishment and much more pessimism.

Samantha got busy at the hearth. She had supplies from several saddlebags from which to cobble together a meal, which would not be elegant but which would be filling. As the federal officers talked to Charles Turner, Ellis went over to stoke the coals for her and to accept another cup of hot coffee which she silently offered him.

He whispered to her that he had told the lawmen where her cache was. He also said he had not volunteered the information, but they had guessed that much. Then, as she turned he said, "All for nothing, Sam. That's counterfeit money. Mister Turner was stealing all the bank's good money and replacing it with counterfeit greenbacks."

She was nonplussed and turned her attention to the federal officers as they talked to Charles Turner. Ellis took over the cooking.

With the exception of Ellis Bowman, everyone in the cabin was listening to what the federal marshals and Charles Turner were saying. Turner did not deny anything. He had not known the lawman were closing in, but he had known for about a month that something like that was inevitable, so he had been getting ready to leave Batesville—in the night on a fast horse if need be.

"One more day," he said. "That was all I needed."

Craig Moore's reply was as dry as old cornhusks. "Mister Turner, one more day wouldn't have helped. What you needed was to leave weeks ago and to not be so damned greedy. Then maybe you could have eluded us. . . . We'd most likely still have got you, though, because we knew who you were, what you look like, and where your private bank account is up in Denver. But it would have been a lot harder than this has been. . . . Mister Turner, I need one more answer from you: Why did you tell the town marshal that money he took from Mister Bowman did not come out of the bank robbery?"

"I needed a little more time and I knew that if I had claimed eleven of that twelve thousand dollars as bank money, Marshal Thompson wouldn't have handed it over real easy—if you knew Thompson as well as I knew him, you'd know that the best way to keep him from raising a fuss would be to let him have Bowman's money. I knew he'd be concentrating on getting rid of Bowman so he could keep the money. It was damned well worth it to me to have the marshal all wrapped up in his own little scheme of theft. . . . And it would have worked too."

Ellis, listening over by the hearth, agreed that it probably would have worked. Otherwise he would not have been invited to ride into the mountains with Thompson, who had made it clear enough what he intended to do.

"How did you convince him it wasn't the bank loot?" Marshal Moore asked.

"That was my clerk's idea. He said to tell Thompson the money stolen from the bank was brand new money from the mint. Will believed me. I made a real act out of getting him to believe me."

"The clerk," said the shorter marshal. "How much of this scheme was his?"

Turner looked up for the first time, and studied Wes Logan's weathered features before he replied in a lowered tone of voice. "It was his idea right from the start. He owned the counterfeiting plates. He had done this sort of thing twice east of the Missouri somewhere. I forget the names of the towns, but he didn't get caught the first time an' the bank had to close its doors. The second time they almost caught him but he headed west. . . . He wasn't a bank clerk by trade, he was an engraver. One of the best I ever saw."

Wes Logan inclined his head about that, then went over to Samantha and smiled at her. "Ma'am, I expect you'd want to shoot me if I just upped and slit open the mattress cover."

She stared at Logan, whose eyes were even with hers. Moore and the other men were looking in her direction, except for Ellis, who was at the stove. But it was his comment that resolved this issue. He said, "Sam, you can use that bootknife of mine to cut the thread if you'd like."

She was horrified by the notion of using the same knife he had killed Marshal Thompson with, so she got a pair of scissors with black-painted grips. She went across to the bunk, hoisted the mattress cover and snipped threads until the first of several greenbacks fell to the floor. They were retrieved by Marshal Moore who handed them to Logan. But he had his magnifying glass in his saddlebags, and their horses were tied back through the timber on the east side of the glade. He left the cabin to ride one back and lead the other two, and during his absence Samantha took hot coffee to Charles Turner. He accepted it gratefully and smiled at her. She did not smile back as she spoke. "Did that money in Marshal Thompson's bank account come from the sale of Sam Hanks' cattle, Mister Turner?"

He sipped the coffee while nodding his head, then he lowered the cup. "Yes."

"And you knew it? You knew he had no right to sell those cattle because they did not belong to him."

Turner lowered his eyes to the contents of his cup. "Samantha, I didn't ask Will any questions. He told me he had a bill of sale to the Hanks cattle. I did not question it."

Samantha's gaze was hardening. "He didn't have a legal bill of sale, and you knew that too, just like you knew there was money in Sam's account when you told me there wasn't. And you told me Sam couldn't read or write, which wasn't true either. I also have his will, Mister Turner. He left me Custer Meadow and all his livestock. You told me there was no will."

Turner shifted on the chair so that he would not have to look at her, and although his coffee cup was still half full, he did not drink from it. Marshal Moore had listened intently.

Ellis was dishing food onto tin plates when he said, "Sam, how about untying the hands of those gents over along the front wall?" Then he slowly winked at her.

She approached the bound men gripping her scissors and Jake, who had reason to know that Samantha could injure a man, shrank back and sputtered. "Lady, all I done was ride with the marshal. That's all me'n Everett done—just our civic duty."

She refused to face either of them as she freed their arms and arose with her back to them. "Yes, that's all you did—your civic duty—just like you did your civic duty when you helped Marshal Thompson round up the Hanks livestock and drive it up north to sell."

As though using one voice both men instantly said, "That wasn't us. That was the marshal an' Arnie."

She whirled on them. "Because they are both dead and can't call you a pair of liars? I've driven cattle. Two men couldn't possibly drive all that livestock through those mountains and you know it!"

The federal officers were owlishly watching Samantha as she helped Ellis put plates on the table. They seemed uncertain about sitting down. Ellis looked at them with understanding and gestured. "Set gents. It's not like Denver, but it'll keep your belt buckles from gettin' hung up on your backbones. She don't bite."

The meal was eaten ravenously. Ellis handed plates to Jake

and Everett, and while he was doing that Everett said, "This here is the luckiest day of Charley Turner's life. If Marshal Thompson was alive and heard how Mister Turner had used him, Mister Turner would never leave this cabin alive."

Ellis said nothing. He took a plate to Charles Turner. The banker looked at it, looked up at Bowman and shook his head. He looked gray and distraught.

When the meal was finished, Craig Moore went outside to look at the horses and have a smoke. Ellis met him out there and the federal officer eyed Bowman thoughtfully. "That money you said the town marshal took from you—where is it?"

"Last I knew it was in that little steel safe in his office down in Batesville."

Moore finished his smoke and ground it underfoot. "Where did you get it?"

"Sold a ranch near Runnymede in Wyoming. The sale deed's in the safe too."

Moore did not question that. "All right. Let's get 'em all on horses and get down out of here. I'd like to reach Batesville by first light."

They returned to the cabin where Wes Logan was stowing the counterfeit money from the bank holdup in his coat pockets. Craig Moore gave the orders. Everyone except Charles Turner obeyed, including Jake, Judd, and Everett, after their bindings had been removed.

Moore stepped aside for everyone to head for the corrals, eyed Turner and rolled his eyes. Ellis nodded understanding. "I'll fetch him," he said, as the lawman turned to follow the others.

Charles Turner was leaning back, head down, the picture of demoralization. Bowman went over to him, touched his shoulder and said, "We're going back now." He pulled up a little stool and sat on it, and while trying to think of something to say, the banker turned his head to fix Bowman with a glassy gaze. "Thirty years wiped out in one day, Mister Bowman. Thirty years."

Ellis could not dispute that and he was too honest by nature to minimize what probably awaited the banker. There were a number of things he could have said, such as the fact that if a man wilfully embarked upon a career of crime, he had to know and accept the risks. But nothing that came to Bowman's mind seemed appropriate, so in the end he arose, tapped the older man again on the shoulder and said, "They're saddlin' the horses," and left the cabin, heading for the pole corrals.

He would have helped Samantha heave her saddle across the tall sorrel horse but before he could reach her, she had already done it and was bending to reach under for the cinch when she looked around, saw who was standing there, and squinted slightly at Ellis. "Mister Moore said it will be a while before the money is returned so its owners can claim it."

Ellis nodded. Moore had told him the same thing.

Samantha fed the latigo through the cinch ring and got things snug before speaking again. "That means perhaps as much as a two-month delay." She turned to face him. "By the end of two months there will be frost at night. You were right, we don't have much time left to make the cabin livable before winter. Until the bank settles with me, I won't have enough to pay your wages, buy a team, and get things organized up there. And I don't want to have to wait another year."

He watched her loop the tag-end of the latigo into its hanger, and leaned on the neck of the horse, regarding her. The horse did not mind. "I expect," he told her, "we could get a loan somewhere. But Sam, the problem is that there are three U.S. marshals who don't think you did the right thing by usin' a gun to rob a bank. I don't know this for a fact but I got a feelin' that when we get back to Batesville they're goin' to lock you up along with the others."

She had no opportunity to respond. One of the deputy

marshals squawked and pointed with a rigid arm at the banker running hard for the timber. Turner had been able to use the cabin to conceal himself until he was too far for the cabin to hide him. By the time one of the federal officers saw him, Charley Turner was already disappearing in the impenetrable forest darkness. Before the men could complete rigging out their animals, Turner was deep in the forest. If it had been daylight they probably would have seen him sooner. Craig Moore was hauling his animal around to be mounted when he snarled at Ellis Bowman. "What'n hell did you leave him alone for?"

As they raced toward the timber, Moore gestured for them to spread out, which they did. Ellis was not aware that Samantha was along until she loped up on his right side, then began to widen the distance between them. She was too far away for him to call out to her to go back. Assuming she would have obeyed.

They made no attempt to be quiet when they got in among the big trees. Marshal Moore paused on a slope, and as one of his companions came close he spoke disgustedly. "It's too dark in here for a man to find his behind with both hands."

The other federal officer said nothing.

They scouted in all directions for an hour before Moore threw up his hands, glared at Ellis and waved everyone back down to open country. His indignation was not lessened any when Samantha said, "We could have ridden within ten feet of him. Any of us."

Moore dismounted holding both reins, gazed back where they had hunted and after a long, bleak moment, spoke to his deputies. "No sense in keepin' it up in the damned dark."

Samantha spoke again in a way not likely to earn Marshal Moore's approval. "We could have waited until daylight before leaving. It was your idea to start back tonight."

Moore lifted his hat, vigorously scratched, lowered the hat and spat, all without looking at Sam or even acting as though he had heard her.

Ellis said, "He won't get far on foot."

Another man added additional encouragement. "We can track him come daylight, Craig. Like the man said, He can't get far on foot. An' he looked sort of soft an' pulpy to me. He won't go far."

Moore still glowered northward. Ellis thought that if Samantha hadn't been there, Craig Moore would have turned the air blue with profanity. He turned his horse without a word, swung astride and led the way back to the cabin. Even as they were off-saddling at the corral he did not speak. As they were heading for the warmth and light of the cabin, he put a smoldering glare on Ellis Bowman.

Not until they were all inside, including the prisoners, and Samantha was feeding kindling into the dying coals, did Ellis notice that the bootknife he had killed Marshal Thompson with and which he had tossed atop the table, was missing. He did not think it was a good time to mention it.

But Marshal Moore was an experienced lawman. As he accepted a cup of black java from Samantha he said, "In the morning when we track him, we got to assume he's armed."

He tasted the coffee and put the cup aside. It was hotter than the hinges of hell. He eyed his companions. "One of you stay here with the prisoners." He meant Deputy Marshal Huddleston.

Ellis took his cup outside and retreated in the direction of the corral. Moore's indignation was justified. He shouldn't have left the banker alone even though the older man had looked about as docile and despondent as a human being could look.

Sam came up, leaned to look in at the horses, and said, "It wasn't your fault."

Ellis sipped hot coffee before replying. "Yeah, it was. But he'd been actin' downright demoralized all afternoon. When I was in there with him while the rest of you were with the horses, he bleated like a goat. Sam, I should have thought he might get desperate enough to try something like this."

She looked up at him. "One fat old man on foot, even in a forest, can't escape from armed men on horseback. Unless he can sprout wings. We'll find him tomorrow. It'll cause a delay; that's about all. As far as I'm concerned, I wish we never had to go back to Batesville. But what worries me much more than what'll happen to me when we get to town is how I'll manage to get things started up on Custer Meadow before the weather changes."

Ellis finished the coffee and let the cup hang at his side as he smiled slightly at her. "Well now, that don't bother me half as much as finding Turner does."

"Why? Don't you care about what I want to do here?"

"Of course I do. That money of mine in Thompson's safe isn't counterfeit." He continued to smile as her eyes widened. "We can use that to do a few things until your money is returned to you from Turner's hidey-hole up in Denver."

She came around very slowly, eyes large and searching. His smile began to fade as they looked steadily at one another. His heart was pounding when the gravelly voice of Wes Logan said, "Hey, you two better get some rest. I'm goin' to stand first watch to make sure that old devil don't try sneakin' back here for a horse."

On the stroll back toward the cabin her fingers sought Ellis's hand and squeezed hard.

# CHAPTER 20
## The Strangers

IN the coldness of predawn as they were rigging out the horses Marshal Moore seemed less disgusted than he had been last night, but Turner's escape still rankled. He looked across his saddle-seat toward Ellis Bowman and quietly said, "You'll never make a lawman."

Ellis looked back. "That's good news. I never wanted to be one."

When they struck out, one deputy marshal, Samantha, and the prisoners remained at the cabin. There were three riders: Ellis Bowman, Marshal Moore and the short deputy named Wes Logan. Each man had a saddlegun as well as a holstered Colt. They had pewter dawnlight all the way to the timber. Up there even though the sun was rising, visibility was poor. It was old timber with spiky tops interwoven to prevent sunlight from reaching all the way to the ground except in a few places.

Logan was a tracker. After an hour of following him as he walked ahead leading his horse, never taking his eyes off the ground, Marshal Moore leaned toward Ellis and said, "Best tracker I ever saw."

Ellis said nothing, but he knew that Moore was making his peace with him.

In the middle distance there was a brief flurry of noise as though some large animal had gone crashing through underbrush, then it stopped and silence settled again. Logan walked back and looked quizzically at Bowman. "You know this country?" he asked, and when Ellis shook his head the short federal deputy turned toward Marshal Moore. "That wasn't no deer," he said.

Moore was looking ahead when he replied. "I'd say maybe it was a bear, Wes. You want me to take the lead?"

Logan shook his head and went back to the point still leading his horse. The very faint imprint of tracks led directly toward the area where the noise had come from. They had ridden no more than half a mile when Logan halted again, this time peering through the ranks of big trees toward distant sunshine where a grassy clearing broke the forest gloom. He did not move even after Moore and Bowman came up and halted. Marshal Moore had a gloved hand resting on the steel butt-plate of his Winchester and he was scowling. "What is it?"

Logan answered without looking around. "We're after one man, Craig; sort of fat and punky." Logan raised an arm slowly. "There was two men across that damned clearing. I saw 'em for a moment or two before they slunk off into the timber."

"Mounted men?"

Logan finally turned. "Yeah. You want me to make a guess? That commotion we heard a while back was made by them two busting out of the forest to lope across the clearin' and go into the forest over yonder."

Moore did not sound very concerned when he said, "Pot hunters. Maybe wolfers."

Logan did not dispute this, he simply said, "Why would they run like hell at the sound of us comin' through the trees?"

Bowman watched Moore's face. The same question had occurred to him. A person would not flee from strangers, unless he had a good reason.

Moore looked down. "Is that where the tracks go?" he asked Logan. Before getting an answer he swung to the ground and held out a hand. "Give me your reins and scout up there a ways on foot. Take your carbine."

After Logan had slipped soundlessly from sight among the huge trees, Marshal Moore wagged his head in Bowman's direction. "If they're renegades, they sure picked good country to hide out in. But we're after one man, not two on horseback—outlaws or no outlaws."

Ellis dismounted. Moore was right about one thing; if someone needed to disappear for a while, this was the best kind of country to do it in.

Logan came back, sank to his haunches leaning on his Winchester, and looked straight up at Marshal Moore. "We got something new, Craig. Just short of that clearin' there was a camp. Coals in the fire-ring are still warm."

Moore acted impatient. "We're not after those two, Wes."

Logan continued to stare upwards. "I think we are. Turner's tracks go toward that camp. It's always hard readin' sign over pine needles, but I'll tell you one thing: His tracks don't go no farther'n that camp. Neither do anyone else's." Logan stood up, considered the quizzical glances he was getting and told them the rest of it. "By my calculations when those fellers busted away from here, they had Turner with them."

Moore snorted. "Three? There was only two fellers across the clearing. You said so. You saw them. If one of them had been carrying double you'd have noticed it, wouldn't you?"

Logan nodded. "Yep. That's my point, Craig. There was *three* men in that camp before Turner got up there. Since neither of the two I saw had Turner ridin' behind his cantle, he must be riding with the third."

"You're sure there was three?"

Logan up-ended his carbine and let it slide into the boot as he said, "Come on. I'll show you."

He was correct—there was sign of three campers in the area of the fire ring. It was an established camp; the needles had been trampled to dust. There was sign of three sets of boot prints in the dust, none matching Turner's prints. Logan pointed in the direction of the grassy clearing. "You want to walk out there in plain sight and look for three sets of horse tracks?"

Marshal Moore shook his head. He wouldn't have ridden

out into the clearing for a hatful of new money, not with three armed strangers somewhere across it, perhaps hiding among the trees over yonder waiting for a target. If they had Turner with them, they sure as hell needed another horse. He spat in the dust and gazed out where sunshine brightened the clearing. "Why would they take Turner with them?"

Ellis made a guess. "Turner knew we'd be after him come morning. He knew we'd be mounted and loaded for bear. After he escaped he probably smelled their campfire smoke last night and came up to them this morning. He'd had all night to work up a scheme. He's one hell of a good schemer. I'd guess he promised them a lot of money to save his hide from us."

Logan grinned. "Counterfeit money?"

Ellis grinned back. "Most likely."

Marshal Moore had reached a decision. He gestured with a gloved hand. "Mount up, Wes. We'll stay among the trees an' circle around the meadow southward. We'd ought to cut their sign again over yonder."

Ellis was toeing into the stirrup when he dryly said, "Yeah. An' if Turner promised them a lot of money to save his hide, he damned well could have promised them more money to get rid of us too."

Neither lawman commented as Wes took the lead again, circling around the clearing and keeping to the deepest forest gloom. He rode with his Winchester across his lap and his eyes searching everything. Wes was out front, not the best place to be if there was an ambush up ahead.

He stopped suddenly, watching something neither Moore nor Bowman could see until its little banner of forest-dust was strung out for about a hundred yards. It was a big dog wolf. It was running hard, tongue lolling, coming directly toward the mounted men. By the time Ellis and Craig Moore could see him, it was clear that it had been badly frightened by something up ahead westward.

The wolf never did see the mounted men; it caught their

scent from a long distance, slammed to a halt, head up, nose testing the air, then it swung due south and was lost to sight within moments.

Ellis leaned on his saddlehorn as he said, "Whatever scairt hell out of him is on the west side of the clearing. Mister Logan, you better be damned careful."

Logan gave Bowman a sardonic look, then eased ahead for a couple of hundred yards before halting long enough to dismount. From this point on he walked ahead carrying his Winchester and leading his horse.

By the time they had the scent of disturbed ancient forest dust in their faces, Ellis Bowman had decided he did not like the way the federal lawmen worked. He rode up beside Moore and said in a barely audible voice, "I'm goin' to split off here. They'll be expecting us as soon as the sun is shining. Whether they're outlaws or wolfers or pot hunters, if Turner has promised them a lot of money to keep us from getting him, they're going to blow you out of your saddle if you keep ridin' the way you're doing. I'm going southward. If I don't find any sign down there, I'll come back northward."

Ellis did not await Marshal Moore's comment but turned away riding downslope without haste. He looked back once but there was no sign of the two federal peace officers.

He did not find any horse tracks but in several places he encountered the dug-in imprints of that frightened dog wolf. He was about as far south as he intended to go when he heard a man's shout from what seemed to be a great distance. He dismounted beside his horse, whipping up his Winchester before it dawned on him the shouting man was not calling to him, he was calling to someone farther up the slope.

It was not possible to make out the words but the voice was harsh and menacing. Ellis swung back astride and continued on a westerly course. Even though the shouting had ended, Ellis had a fair idea of the man's location as he worked back and forth among huge old overripe pines and firs climbing northward up the gradual slope.

He was very aware of his own peril. Whoever the men were who had saved Turner from capture, they certainly knew three riders had been seeking the banker, not two. If they'd caught sight of the marshals by now, they knew he had split off from them. That would mean he was stalking them from a different direction.

How they would react to this was not altogether predictable, but they would be waiting for him.

The second time that man with the growly voice shouted, Ellis heard him distinctly: "You boys better turn back. You ain't goin' to get holt of Turner, and if you keep this up you're goin' to wish you'd gone back."

Ellis halted at the dogleg of a little creek and let his animal tank up. He frowned as he considered that shouted warning. A fugitive from the law in a country that was ideal for a successful bushwhacking, wouldn't yell a warning—he'd start shooting. At the very least he'd catch Logan and Moore by surprise and capture them.

Either Logan or Moore yelled back. It was hard to distinguish voices in a forest. Whoever it was called out that he was a federal marshal with a warrant for Charles Turner's arrest. The answers he got back came from three different voices, all loudly and profanely derisive. The loudest man said, "Sure you're federal lawmen. An' I'm the President of the United States. Turn around, boys, while you're still able, and don't stop until you're back down in flat country."

Ellis left his horse tied in dark shade not far from the little creek and started walking in the direction of those derisive voices, his Winchester crooked in his arm.

It did not seem that the men he was stalking knew one of Turner's pursuers was not with the other two. Apparently, Logan and Moore were well enough hidden among the close-spaced big trees to conceal this fact.

Ellis was sweating hard and had to pause to catch his

breath; because although the slope he was walking up was not at all steep, Bowman was a horseman and horsemen never went anywhere on foot in open country if they could possibly avoid it.

While slipping between two huge fir trees, he saw tethered horses, three of them, which corroborated what he suspected. After a moment of hesitation he turned in the direction of the animals. His intention was to cut them loose and put the men protecting Charles Turner on foot.

He was within twenty feet of the horses, and the animals had either detected movement among the trees or had caught man-scent, but in either event they were standing motionless, ears forward, peering in his direction. Bowman stopped beside a tree and studied the horses.

Each one wore old, battered equipment. Each one had an empty carbine boot, a blanketroll behind the saddle, big old army saddlebags, and a thick, tightly-rolled bundle of silver-tan wolf hides. He peered left and right, saw nothing, heard nothing and made a correct judgment: the men into whose camp Charley Turner had breathlessly stumbled were wolfers. It was a little early in the year for taking hides; heat made hair slip. Professional wolfers would know that. It occurred to him that these wolfers had probably taken the hides at higher elevations where it was colder and had been making a leisurely descent to lower territory where there would be towns and hide buyers.

He was still wasting time speculating when something struck him between the shoulderblades with the force of a mule-kick, knocking him to his knees. He lost the Winchester and was fighting for breath when a pair of thick legs in dirty, faded trousers came around where he could see them.

He was struggling for breath, gasping and choking when a heavily-bearded dark man leaned, wrenched his sixgun away and tossed it. As breath began to return, the pain started. He fell forward on his hands and knees and hung there like a gut-shot bear as his assailant said, "You know him?" Ellis recognized the voice that answered, but as though from a distance. "Yes. He's one of them. His name's Bowman. He's the one that made the plan to kill me, hide my carcass, then go down in the night and empty the bank's safe."

The swarthy, bearded man spoke musingly. "You can't rightly blame him, Mister Turner. Fifty-five thousand dollars is an awful lot of money. Well, this changes things. You go back an' tell my partners what we caught. I'll set here with Mister Bowman. Tell 'em I think they'd better throw a few shots to scatter them other two, then we better get astride and run for it."

Ellis's backache was a fiery knot of pain as his breath returned and his mind began to clear. He remained head hung down on all fours as he heard the banker departing in haste. His assailant hunkered down holding a saddlegun across his lap and quietly said, "Hey, deputy marshal, let's see your badge."

Ellis was still sucking air in loud sweeps and did not raise his head, so the lean, bearded man caught him by the hair and roughly forced his head up. The man had small, very dark eyes and a nearly hidden wide, lipless, cruel mouth. He leaned to scowl into Ellis's face. "Show me your badge, or I'll break your neck."

Ellis winced, in so much pain he could hardly speak. "I don't have a badge," he croaked.

The swarthy man released his grip on Bowman's scalp and smiled harshly. "Never thought you did have. Or them other fellers either. Mister Turner told us who you are. Bank robbers."

Ellis said nothing. His head was throbbing where the stranger's grip had aggravated his earlier head wound. He did not care whether the man thought he was a bank robber or not; he only cared that his strength would return and the terrible hurt in his back would fade away.

The swarthy man said, "You got any chawin' tobacco?"

Ellis unsteadily wagged his head. "Don't chew." He dug in

hard with his heels, eased his weight off his hands and catapulted straight into the bearded man, whose face showed abrupt astonishment. The wolfer used his left hand to keep Bowman off while reaching for his hip-holster with his right hand. Ellis used both hands; he missed a strike at the bearded man's face and fired his other hand, which landed on the wolfer's throat. The dark man made barking, choking sounds and raised both hands to protect himself. He was hurt but he was also as tough as rawhide. It went with his trade. He flopped sideways and kicked savagely with both feet.

Ellis was knocked off balance when one boot connected with his hip. By the time he swung forward again the wolfer was springing to his feet.

Ellis lept up in desperation. The injured wolfer was reaching toward his holster again. Ellis was too distant to use fists so he kicked out in desperation, caught the wolfer on the kneecap causing him to crumple when one leg failed to support him.

Ellis launched himself with both fists flailing. There was no particular skill to his attack but it was effective. He beat the wolfer to the ground and was yanking out the man's sixgun when someone roared at him from one side. Ellis had the gun in his hand as he twisted to look.

The other two wolfers and Charley Turner were standing thirty feet away. One wolfer raised his carbine and snugged it back. Ellis opened his hand to let the sixgun drop, and slowly straightened up.

Now, with nausea and back pain gripping him, the fierce and angry men with Winchesters swam in his vision.

# CHAPTER 21
## "Dead Sure"

THE two wolfers beat him mercilessly. And although he tried to see through the blur and ignore the crippling pain, each time he twisted or tried to stand straight, he was defenseless against their onslaught. When he finally dropped senseless to the ground, they stopped—panting, cursing, dripping sweat.

Charles Turner stood by and watched, his face showing fear and horror. He had seen men beaten before, but never like this.

They helped the injured wolfer up. One of them said, "How'd you let that son of a bitch jump you?"

The swarthy man ignored the question and looking across the glade, said, "Hell, we better get away from here."

Turner edged closer but avoided looking at Ellis, lying inert in the grass. The wolfer who was anxious to leave went back to the saddle stock and growled at his companions to hurry.

They were getting ready to mount when the man who had been carrying Turner behind his saddle said sourly, "Someone else take Mister Turner for a change." Five seconds later a gunshot sounded from somewhere over yonder to the east. The wolfers paused. Then the swarthy man said, "They're still over there. I think we got to find their animals."

His two companions thought differently. One of them spoke curtly. "Hell with them an' their horses. We'll steal one when we get down out of here on our way to the bank."

Two more gunshots sounded, but southward, not eastward across the meadow. The swarthy man swung his head in both directions and mounted hastily. "Go west. They're comin' around the glade to the south," he said.

The shortest of the wolfers, a lean, sinewy older man frowned. "What in the hell are they shootin' at; they can't see us."

No one answered him as his companions gathered reins and faced due west. They were threading their way among the trees, with Charley Turner, when three more gunshots echoed. The man he was riding behind twisted to glare. "Why don't they quit? Nobody can shoot straight in a damned dark forest."

There was no more gunfire but as the wolfers were widening the distances, a muffled shout came vaguely to them, the words indistinguishable. There were more shouts, then silence.

An hour later the swarthy man glared murderously in Turner's direction and broke the silence. "You sure better have told us the truth, mister."

Turner bleated an answer. "I did exactly that. Fifty-five thousand in the vault. Only two men on earth know the combination. Me an' my clerk. You'll get it, but we daren't approach town in daylight. And if they're tracking us, sure as hell they'll see us once we reach open country."

The small, older man smiled. "Mister Turner, we been outsmartin' the smartest animal on four feet. We know ambushes better'n anyone alive."

Nothing more was said until the lead wolfer abruptly yanked his horse to a dead stop. The others swung left and right to come up beside him. The lead rider put both hands atop the saddlehorn and stared. "Six of 'em. There wasn't but three of them other fellers."

His companions sat alert and silent, staring at the motionless horsemen arranged across open timber ahead. The swarthy wolfer said, "Cattlemen?"

The lead rider replied scornfully. "In a damned forest where cattle don't go because there ain't no grass?"

"Well, who then? Sure as hell they aren't those other fellers. . . . Act relaxed. Talk to them."

The lead man said softly, "They don't look friendly." Then he called ahead, "Howdy, gents. You just passin' through like us?"

He was answered by a frail-appearing old man riding a bull-built, mule-nosed bay horse. "My name's Cuthbert," he told the wolfers, barely raising his voice. "We're from Batesville. These here gents are the town blacksmith, his apprentice, the liveryman an' his dayman. And that there rider on the sorrel horse is Sam Hanks. It's not her real name but she's been using it, which is all right with us." Having said that, the Batesville apothecary paused before adding a little more. "Hello, Mister Turner. After Miss Hanks and a deputy marshal brought some prisoners in the town folks got to worrying about you, wandering around out here."

The burly blacksmith's apprentice smiled and rubbed one massive fist against the palm of his other hand, making it glaringly clear how much he and the others wanted to get their hands on Turner.

Cuthbert continued speaking quietly, his eyes fixed upon the banker. "Who are these gents, Charley?"

The swarthy wolfer replied. "We're trappers. We found Mister Turner wanderin' around up here without a horse." He smiled disarmingly. His right hand was within inches of his hip-holster. "We was takin' him back to Batesville."

At that moment a rider emerged from the trees, slowly because he had been reading the sign left by the wolfers. Once in the clearing, Moore rode quickly enough to join the gathering. He nodded at the deputy marshal and Samantha, then said, "These three come within an ace of beatin' Bowman to death back yonder. Logan, one of the deputy marshals, stayed back with him."

Samantha abruptly rode off, spurring her horse through the trees in the direction of the glade as U.S. Marshal Craig Moore swung to the ground and pulled out his carbine.

Everyone knew whatever was going to happen next was up to the wolfers. If they made a fight out of it, they were going to hell. Old Cuthbert spoke quietly to them. "Dismount, gents, get rid of your guns. Did Mister Turner promise to pay you for takin' his side? If he did, there's somethin' you might want to know. The money in his bank is counterfeit."

The wolfers were swinging to the ground. They turned to look at Charley Turner. He tried a lopsided smile. His face was red. He did not have to admit anything; his face did it for him. The swarthy wolfer said, "You son of a bitch," drawing and firing his handgun as he spoke. Then all hell busted loose.

The saloonman and Marshal Moore dived for cover. They were behind the wolfers. When the noise stopped two wolfers and Charley Turner were heaped close to one another, bullet-riddled, a third wolfer had been grazed on the arm, and the town possemen were fighting panicked horses.

Marshal Moore strode ahead and proded the corpses with his Winchester barrel. He seemed to be the calmest man among them. He said, "Here's something for you fellers to ponder over. There are five bullet holes in Turner an' he not only wasn't armed but he didn't start the fight." Before anyone could comment about this, Moore addressed the townsmen again. "If my deputy and Sam Hanks were with you, who'n hell is back in town watching the prisoners.

The town liveryman, the first to get his horse talked down, answered. "When that deputy and Sam Hanks didn't hear nothing from you, they decided to bring the prisoners to town and get help. We rounded up some possemen, left two at the jail on guard, and headed out here."

Marshal Moore looked around, then back. "All right. We got one live wolfer and two dead men. Let's get the hell back down out of here and over to Batesville. We'll pick up Bowman and Logan on the way. Lend a hand, gents."

The two dead wolfers were the swarthy man and the lead rider, a gangling, unwashed, unshorn and unshaved man.

The surviving wolfer was the older man. He told them the names of his companions. His own name was Hiram Muller.

Moore took the lead over his backtrail. The others rode silently behind him single file, weaving among the trees like a very large snake with a lot of legs. The dead men undulated inertly with the cadence of the horses they were lashed to.

As they were nearing the clearing, a townsman said, "What in the holy hell did that wolfer pull a gun for?"

Old Cuthbert answered quietly. "For the same reason one bloody-hand Indian would charge into a whole regiment of cavalry: crazy."

The topic died there. Whether the old man's assessment was too simple or not was not going to be argued. They had the glade in sight. Moore stood in his stirrups. He saw Logan but there was no sign of Samantha, her horse or Bowman. He rode to the spot where there was torn earth, trampled grass and drying blood. Wes Logan was standing there holding the reins to his horse. He had been left behind to do what he could for Bowman. He did not say a word as he counted the riders coming toward him from the forest, looked longest at the belly-down corpses, then squinted, expectorated and nodded to Marshal Moore. "Sounded like a small war," he said dryly.

Moore did not dismount. "More like a massacre," he replied, and looked ahead. "Did she take him out of here?"

Logan stood hipshot trailing the reins to his horse. "Yeah. It took both of us to get him up on her horse. She rode behind holding onto him."

"Was he all right?"

Logan looked steadily at Marshal Moore. "Yeah. For a man who's been kicked, clubbed and beat unconscious, he was just fine." Logan turned, swung into his saddle, and as the cavalcade started on across the glade, he fell in beside the saloonman, who gave him a detailed account of the fight. Logan turned to stare at the flopping head of the swarthy wolfer, then at the surviving wolfer, spat and straightened forward in the saddle. "The three of them against eight of you?"

The saloonman nodded and met the lawman's gaze. "You bein' a lawman an' all, does it make any sense to you?"

Logan shrugged, faced forward and rode in silence.

The dust of Samantha's passage still hung in the sun-dappled forest. By now it was a well-marked trail. The townsmen were sore and dog-tired. With the exception of the liveryman none of them had done much saddlebacking over the years, and since leaving Batesville they had ridden through country that punished both horses and men.

Occasionally Marshal Moore glanced over his shoulder. Otherwise he rode the way men do who have a fixed objective in mind and do not welcome diversions.

By the time they got down to Samantha's cabin, with Moore still in the lead, the townsmen had put in a lot of miles and a lot of hours. They piled off to spring their knees and look around. Samantha and Bowman were not there. Logan scouted around and returned shaking his head. "She took him to town, sure as hell."

Marshal Moore got them back astride and led off in the direction of open country. He knew Bowman must not have been seriously injured or she would not have kept going. The townsmen were sore, tired, and hungry. By the time they could see distant rooftops, the day was drawing to a close.

When the party rode down Batesville's main street, people appeared on both sides of the road to stare and mutter among themselves. All kinds of stories had been going around since the possemen left town with Sam Hanks and the deputy marshal.

Now, as people stood like statues watching the riders pass, a few recognized Craig Moore in the lead. Everyone knew the other horsemen except for the live and dead wolfers, and Wes Logan.

The man who operated the general store came out to watch, accompanied by his wizened old clerk. The proprietor was bleak-faced. He had not seen the other federal deputy enter town earlier with two blanket-shrouded corpses, but his clerk had heard a rumor that one of those dead men was Will Thompson. Now, as the horsemen rode south toward the livery barn, the storekeeper spoke aside to his clerk. "What the hell is going on?"

The clerk's reply was succinct. "Most likely we'll hear all about it tomorrow."

The storekeeper snorted. "Yeah! Talk! That's what folks do when they don't know anythin' but won't admit it. I don't believe any of those rumors."

The clerk shrugged thin shoulders. "The feller who told me about Thompson said he saw the body."

The merchant considered that and because his clerk was a truthful man, he simply said, "Maybe. An' maybe not."

The clerk sniffed. "Ain't no terrible loss. Did you recognize one of them dead men who just went past?"

"No. Did you?"

"Yes. Charley Turner."

The storekeeper gave a little start then turned an incredulous stare toward his clerk. "No. Are you sure?"

"Dead sure."

# CHAPTER 22
# Loose Ends And Weary Bones

THE Batesville jailhouse had not been built to accommodate many people, so it was crowded when the saloonman and the blacksmith brought Charley Turner's clerk up out of the cell-room to stand blinking in lamplight. He recognized most of the motionless, armed men awaiting him. Someone slammed the cell-room door, shoved the clerk toward the wall and stood between him and the wallrack of guns. The craggy blacksmith looked icily at the clerk, his face set in an expression of uncompromising judgment. Wes Logan took the surviving wolfer by the arm and shoved him down into the cell-room to be locked in, and returned to join the others.

All three federal officers were there as were the six town-riders and at least eight local men, merchants for the most part. Haggard and bruised-looking Ellis Bowman was there as was Samantha Coe. They had come to town before Moore and the others, but they had been careful not to be seen by prying townspeople as they took the back way to her residence. She and Bowman were the only people closely involved with all that had happened up yonder who looked like they'd eaten and washed.

Marshal Moore told the bank clerk in a sepulchral voice what Charles Turner had said about counterfeiting, and the clerk looked for something to sit on before answering.

He was a nondescript individual with a receding chin, ferret-eyes and a paleness from being indoors most of the time. He had brown eyes behind glasses with thick lenses. What Bowman remembered about the man was his attitude at the bank the only other time they had met. The clerk never smiled and exuded an attitude of annoying superiority.

For a moment it appeared the clerk would deny the things Charles Turner had said. What may have made him waver were the quiet, stone-hard faces turned in his direction. It was clear that none of the grim-faced men in the crowded little office doubted what Turner had said, so the clerk had one of two choices; tell the truth or try lying. Lying could possibly get him hurt or killed, whereas the truth would only land him in a federal prison, so he told the truth.

He admitted that the plates for counterfeiting bank notes were his. He had engraved them in Ohio, had used them extensively all the way out to Batesville. Moore and the others already knew this but the one thing they didn't know was where the plates were hidden. But Moore was careful not to press him too hard, too fast.

Old Cuthbert, the apothecary, mentioned something that particularly interested him. "How much trouble did you have talking Charley Turner into goin' into the counterfeiting business with you?"

The clerk removed his glasses, polished them vigorously with a blue handkerchief, hooked them back into place and peered around owlishly as he relied. "None at all, Mister Cuthbert, after I showed him how rich he could become in so short a length of time."

"What was your cut?" Moore asked.

The clerk's eyes jumped from Cuthbert's face to Moore's, and back as he replied. "Twenty percent. We'd replace every deposit with the counterfeit money, split the good money— eighty percent to him, twenty percent to me."

"What did you do with it?"

"It's hidden with the plates."

Marshal Moore made a show of yawning, as if whatever the clerk said was of no particular interest to him. Casually, he asked, "Where?"

The clerk stared blankly at Moore. It seemed to dawn on him suddenly that he was in a good bargaining position.

Finally, Moore raised his eyes to the others. "It's been a long day, gents. I'm worn down to a nubbin. Suppose we lock this feller back in his cell and head for supper and bed. Deputy Huddleston will stand guard first. If you got more questions for the prisoner, come back in the morning." He and Logan locked the clerk in a cell. As everyone else was leaving, Moore took Huddleston aside and whispered something.

Outside, the blacksmith stood balefully regarding the jail door. He worked hard for his money, like everyone else, and now it seemed that he and all the merchants and townspeople were holding worthless notes put into circulation by Turner and the clerk. The blacksmith looked at the others and said, "Maybe we'll get our savings back, and maybe we won't. For my part, gents, I'd as soon take this son of a bitch out back and shoot him. Nothing I hate worse'n a thief."

Before anyone else replied Ellis, who did not want another killing, spoke up. "You'll get it back. Marshal Moore was sure of that."

The jail door opened suddenly. Moore and Logan stood, filling the doorway and the crowd stepped back instinctively.

"Is there something more you gents want?" Moore asked pointedly. He surveyed the group, staring hard into each face.

Samantha and Ellis did not speak, but both looked at the blacksmith. Catching their cue, Moore turned to the self-appointed leader and repeated, "Is there something you want?"

The others began to disperse, leaving the blacksmith on his own to face Moore. He sucked his teeth in dismay and walked away.

"You folks care to join us for dinner?" Samantha asked as Moore and Logan stepped away from the doorway.

"Uh, no thanks," Moore said uneasily. "We have a few

things to take care of first." He and Logan headed down the street.

Ellis walked Samantha home.

When they reached her home she asked, "Do you think we should look for a team and wagon tomorrow, or just rest for a day or two?"

He almost grinned. She would never be anything but direct and practical. With her face scrubbed it looked as clean as new money and ten times prettier. He said, "Well, suppose I hunt you up when I've got my sleep out. Maybe not very early." He was bone-tired and had been functioning on just willpower for the last ten hours.

She accepted that. "All right." She went to the door, then faced him again as though she had something particular and private to tell him. He waited but all she did was smile and close the door.

Ellis headed for the boardinghouse, but for a brief moment he considered going back to the jail. With Thompson dead and with no inkling where he might have written down the combination to the steel safe, it appeared to Ellis that the only way he was going to get his moneybelt back was to hire the blacksmith to cut the door off with tools and heat. For now, though, he decided his money was probably as safe inside the steel box as it would be anywhere else, and made his way to the roominghouse.

# CHAPTER 23
## Starting Over

ELLIS did not have breakfast at the roominghouse because he did not even open his eyes until ten o'clock. He ate down at the cafe, which was still lively with jumbled facts, wild flights of fancy, and pure imaginings.

While the five or six diners who were at the counter when Bowman sat down knew who he was, and that he had been up to his gullet in the whole darned mess, none of them tried to strike up a conversation. Not even when Samantha Coe appeared in the doorway, and saw him shoveling in food. She sat down beside him and asked for a cup of coffee.

Ellis turned, detecting the scent of lilac before he saw her. She was no longer dressed as she had been when he had last seen her. She was now dressed for work. The only thing she lacked was that old hat which had been part of her masculine disguise when they had first met—and she had left him there to be caught, and had stolen his horse to boot.

She smiled winsomely. "You shaved."

He went back to his meal. "Yeah. Took an all-over bath too."

"Did you sleep well?"

"Like a dead man. You?"

"Very well."

"Have you eaten?"

"Yes. Hours ago." She drained the coffee cup and put it aside. "The liveryman has three teams of harness animals to show you, when you're finished here. . . . No need to hurry, Ellis."

He chewed, swallowed, turned, and gazed at her. She gave him that bright smile again. He shook his head and went back to his meal. When she said no need to hurry, she meant hurry up. He was learning.

They were leaving the cafe when they met deputy Wes Logan outside the door. He had not shaved and, in fact, he was still wearing the same clothes he'd had on for several days now, but he smiled at them when they halted, and he said, "Morning, ma'am, Ellis. Don't reckon you heard about what happened last night after you left the jail?"

Ellis and Samantha were puzzled. Had the blacksmith and the others gone back and made trouble?

"What happened?" asked Ellis.

Logan took them aside and spoke in hushed tones. "Marshal Moore figured we'd never get that wiley old clerk to tell us where the plates and his share of the money was. So Huddleston conveniently let him escape—"

Samantha gasped and clutched Ellis's arm.

"Now, hold on," Logan said quickly. "Marshal and me was never more than a stone's throw from him. We tailed him, and when he got the plates we grabbed him. All the town's money has been recovered, but you'll understand that the marshal doesn't want any of this talked about until we safely get the plates, the money, and the prisoner out of town."

"But the town *will* get the money back?" asked Ellis. "There's no question of that?"

"No question at all," he replied. Then he turned toward Samantha. "But there is something else I expect you'd like to know, ma'am. Marshal Moore, me, and deputy Huddleston got to talking about you last night. About you 'borrowing' that money from the bank. We come to the conclusion that getting all the rest of this mess sorted out and sifted through will mean we got to set down and write a report that'll maybe take up fifteen or twenty pages, and since none of us likes writing reports, an' since this here one is goin' to be a real tangle of a problem, we figured it'd be best just to leave you out of it. It's goin' to be hard enough as it is, and besides that, you gave the money back, even though it was only counterfeit, and like Craig said, you done us more good than harm."

Having said all that, Wes Logan held out his hand. Samantha shook it. He then did the same for Ellis, and when that little ritual had been completed, Logan nodded and entered the cafe.

On their way down to the livery barn Ellis was thoughtfully silent for half the distance, until Samantha looked around and spoke. "I think what just happened proves a point. Worrying about something makes it seem much worse than it will be."

Ellis nodded without commenting.

The liveryman was sitting in a tipped-back chair out front of his business establishment, and as they came up he nodded without speaking and led the way out back to one of his corrals.

He peered in at a matched pair of dappled grays as he spoke. "They're broke to pack, to drive, an' they'll work in heavy harness or drivin' harness. They're four years old, a mite young for knowin' all they know." He paused to look at Ellis. "As near as I could figure out they don't have any bad habits, an' I drove 'em, made 'em pull, and—see there—even had 'em shod because I figured there had to be a hole in them somewhere. Darned if I could make them make a mistake."

Ellis leaned to study the big matched pair. He didn't have to mouth them. If they'd been older than the liveryman had said, their dapples would have been fading. If they'd been nine or ten, they would have been a uniform gray-white with no trace of the dapples.

Their legs were good, no splints, the customary blemish on young horses that are made to work too hard. They had good heads and fine eyes. They did not even have scars from collar sores.

The liveryman misinterpreted Ellis's long silence and straightened up. "There's another pair, big bays, older but honest, big animals. An' a nice pair of Mexican mules. Strong as any horse livin'. A little scary because I expect they been beat—Mexicans are known for that." The liveryman would have walked to the other corrals to show the bays and mules. While he waited for Ellis to straighten up off the corral poles he also said, "I got to tell you, Mister Bowman, unless a man's got good corrals and knows mules, he's better off to buy horses. Mules is like women—smarter'n horses and devious. Sly and treacherous even when they're—" He let it trail off, getting red in the face because of his tactlessness. Even his ears got red.

Ellis pulled back slowly, faced the liveryman as though the man's incredible gaffe was the most normal thing in the world, and said, "How much for the grays?"

Samantha cleared her throat and although the liveryman would not look around at her, he seemed to flinch at the sound she made. "Forty dollars a head, Mister Bowman, an' if you aren't figurin' on takin' them clean out of the country—if they turn up bad some way you can fetch them back and I'll give you your forty dollars back. . . . An' that's something' I ain't in the habit of doing. It's just that you . . . an' Miss Coe . . . done so much for the folks here in—"

"Throw in a couple of halters and we'll take them," stated Ellis.

The liveryman turned, avoiding eye-contact with Samantha, and went scuttling back into the barn for a pair of halters and lead ropes.

Ellis leaned on the corral stringers watching her. "You like them?" he asked.

"Yes indeed. Those were the animals I was hoping you'd pick." She leaned on the rail, looking in at the grays. "We wouldn't want the mules, would we?"

He kept a poker-faced expression when he replied. "No ma'am."

She smiled sweetly at him. "Because we don't have good corrals up there yet. That's the only reason, isn't it?"

"Oh yes indeed, ma'am. That'd be the only reason. What other reason could there be?"

She continued to smile at him. "Because they're like women—smarter than horses. Just barely though, wouldn't you say?"

Ellis rubbed his jaw watching the rear barn entrance for the liveryman to reappear. It was taking him a long time to find two halters and two shanks. "I can't rightly say, Sam. I never had much truck with mules."

"Or women," she said sweetly.

"Yes'm. Or women. I'd have to go on the liveryman's word, he seems to have had experience with both women and mules."

Her smile remained. "Do you suppose an intelligent mule could open Will Thompson's safe?"

He lowered his eyes to her face. The sweet smile lingered but the gray eyes were unwaveringly still and pensive. He said, "Sam, he just shot off his mouth. He never impressed me as much of a hand anyway. Forget it, he's a fool who don't think before he talks."

She nodded and allowed the smile to fade. "I know he's a fool. I've known him a lot longer than you have. But he's never been so tactless before."

"All right, we agree he's a fool, an' we bought our big horses. . . . What about Thompson's safe?"

"I have the combination."

He gazed at her unmindful of the rising sun or anything else. "How did you get the combination?"

"I've known it for years. I found the combination on a scrap of paper in a little tin box of other papers that belonged to my father. You see, my father sold Marshal Thompson that safe."

The liveryman did not return. He sent his dayman out with the halters and ropes. Because the dayman had not been told what had happened out back as he handed over the halters he said, "The boss had to go up to the saloon. He left me to finish up here with you folks."

Ellis accepted the ropes and halters and asked about pack outfits. The dayman pointed in the direction of the general store. "They got five or six sets. Good outfits too; none of them little short Mex pack-trees made out of cottonwood that fit burros and ruin the backs of horses."

They left the halters draped on a corral post, told the dayman they'd be back directly, and went up the back alley to the jailhouse. The rear door was barred from the inside, but their rattling of the door brought Moore. He opened the door, then jerked his head for them to enter and rebarred the door after them.

Ellis told Moore that Logan had explained everything and that they had come to get the money that belonged to Ellis. Moore watched them go behind the desk, kneel before the safe, and when Samantha went to work on the dial the marshal walked over scowling. But he said nothing until she pulled the door open and Ellis retrieved his moneybelt, emptied the greenbacks atop the desk, and began counting.

Later in the afternoon, Ellis and Samantha went to the emporium, looked at the pack outfits, selected two, both made from back leather, no neck of belly leather, paid for them, and returned to the barn to pay for the dapple grays. Then they returned to the roadway and halted out there. Ellis squinted skyward, looked at her and said, "By the time we get supplies and tools and whatnot, it'll be kind of late to start for the meadow, Sam."

She nodded about that even though she wanted to strike out.

He studied her expression. "We could get loaded about sunup in the morning an' make it up there with lots of daylight left."

She nodded about that too, without looking up at him.

He shifted stance, shot another look at the position of the sun, and blew out a big sigh. "All right. Let's go back to the store and buy what we'll need. . . . Are you any good at making baking powder biscuits by moonlight, Sam?"

Her eyes came up. "Yes, even if there isn't a moon. I can make a meal by firelight." She smiled at him. "But you'd rather wait until morning so we'll wait. Besides, I'm sure your back hurts."

He did not deny that. But all he said was: "Maybe. But if you can make decent biscuits by moonlight, why then I expect you could do it by lamplight. . . . Supper this evening at your house?"

She looked steadily at him.

He reddened slightly. "So's we can go over the list of what we have bought and make plumb sure we're not forgettin' something, because it's a long trip back if we have. That's all. Well, and a homecooked meal."

She was gazing in the direction of the emporium when she agreed, and led off across the road.

They did not have a list, but he knew which tools they would need and she knew which varieties of tinned food they would need. For once the storekeeper did not object to waiting on customers a half hour after he would normally have closed his store for the night. He had seen what was inside the pockets of that moneybelt.

The storekeeper even helped them load the *alforjas,* and the dayman down at the barn promised to lock the harness-room door so the loaded pack boxes would be safe until morning. If anyone wondered about what Bowman and Samantha Coe were doing, they were discreetly quiet about it, at least in the presence of Samantha and Ellis. What they told their wives at home, or discussed among themselves up at The Waterhole Saloon, was likely to be lively and speculative.

The sun had departed, and shadows softened the rough corners of Batesville's buildings. A fragrant little evening breeze came southward from the mountains to stir a little dust in the main thoroughfare and cause undulations among the laden clotheslines, by the time Samantha took Ellis Bowman down the sideroad where her residence was located.

She was nervous but hid it well.

When she brought him coffee in the parlor from the kitchen where she had gone to prepare supper, he accepted the cup as he said, "Sam, what you got here is what most folks want and work toward. That old log house up yonder, even after we get it worked over, most likely won't be this nice—and down here you got stores just around the corner."

She agreed. "It is a matter of choosing between inconveniences, Ellis. Down here, as you said, there are stores. But, down here, there are no big trees, meadow, open country, the silence and the beauty that feeds a person's soul. So—now and then—I'd rather live there and put up with the trip down here occasionally for supplies."

"You are forgetting something, Sam."

"What."

"The work. . . . From sunup to sundown, aches and bruises and disappointments, fallin' asleep at the supper table. . . ."

She looked up at him, wonderingly. "After all we've been through, you don't think I should do it?"

He detected no hint of indecision in her voice. "Sam, I think you should do whatever matters most to you."

She smiled a little. "Custer Meadow matters most to me."

He grinned. He had not expected any other reply. "Just so's you'll know," he said, and gestured. "You're goin' to burn those biscuits."

She hastened to the kitchen, was out of his sight briefly, then poked her head around the doorway. "What do you want most, Ellis?"

He regarded her shiny nose and perfectly proportioned features as he answered. "Custer Meadow." As her head drew back from his sight he turned toward a window and stood gazing beyond into starlighted darkness. He did not believe he had told her the whole truth. Something like Custer Meadow was indeed what he had thought of so many times while forking hay to cattle through a couple of feet of Wyoming snow, even though he had not been convinced he would ever find that kind of country no matter how much riding he did.

But he knew himself well enough to realize that it was not just Custer Meadow that he wanted—now. A month back it would have been, but it was not what he wanted now. Well, it was not *all* he wanted now.

She called him to supper at the kitchen table. It was the first meal they had eaten alone together, not counting that first night at her cabin in the glade when he had thought she was a man. He did not want to particularly recall that night. She probably did not want to recall it either. Maybe someday, but not this evening.

She was an excellent cook, which did not really surprise him. She could make biscuits so light he was ashamed of himself for eating so many.

She laughed at his expression when the biscuit dish was empty. She also learned something: In the future when she baked biscuits for him, she would make three times as many as she would ordinarily bake for just two people.

After supper they went out front. She sat on the porch swing and he got settled on the steps with his back to an overhang upright. They talked for an hour, of plans, of projections, of the order of things to be undertaken before full winter arrived, and he eventually left her to head for the roominghouse, and she sat perfectly still on the porch watching him until he was out of sight.

But she knew he'd be back. And so did he.

If you have enjoyed this book and would like to receive details of other Walker Western titles, please write to:

Western Editor
Walker and Company
720 Fifth Avenue
New York, NY 10019